"Give Me Credit For A Little Style, Shelby.

"I certainly wouldn't want to consummate our relationship in a rathole like the Seagull Motel."

Her heart lurched, and she snatched her hand away from him. "We're not going to *consummate* our relationship anywhere, Garrett McGrath. We don't even have a relationship."

"Don't we?"

"Certainly not!" she insisted swiftly and forcefully. Too swiftly and forcefully, she realized. "And don't you dare try to come back with that overused quotation about 'the lady doth protest too much'!"

"I don't have to. You're doing an excellent job of it on your own."

"An excellent job of what?"

"Of verifying that we do indeed have a relationship. One that most certainly will be consummated in time."

Dear Reader,

Welcome once again to Silhouette Desire! Enter into a world of powerful love and sensuous romance, a world where your most passionate fantasies come true.

September begins with a sexy, sassy MAN OF THE MONTH, *Family Feud* by Barbara Boswell, a writer you've clearly indicated is one of your favorites.

And just as exciting—if you loved Joan Johnston's fantastic HAWK'S WAY series, then don't miss CHILDREN OF HAWK'S WAY, beginning with *The Unforgiving Bride*.

The month is completed with stories from Lass Small, Karen Leabo, Beverly Barton and Carla Cassidy. *Next* month, look for a MAN OF THE MONTH by Annette Broadrick *and* the continuation of Joan Hohl's BIG, BAD WOLFE series.

So, relax, read, enjoy...and fall in love all over again with Silhouette Desire.

Sincerely yours,

Lucia Macro
Senior Editor

Please address questions and book requests to:
Silhouette Reader Service
U.S.: 3010 Walden Ave., P.O. Box 1325, Buffalo, NY 14269
Canadian: P.O. Box 609, Fort Erie, Ont. L2A 5X3

BARBARA BOSWELL
FAMILY FEUD

SILHOUETTE *Desire*®

Published by Silhouette Books

America's Publisher of Contemporary Romance

SILHOUETTE BOOKS

ISBN 0-373-05877-2

FAMILY FEUD

Books by Barbara Boswell

BARBARA BOSWELL

loves writing about families. "I guess family has been a big influence on my writing," she says. "I particularly enjoy writing about how my characters' family relationships affect them."

When Barbara isn't writing and reading, she's spending time with her *own* family—her husband, three daughters and three cats, whom she concedes are the true bosses of their home! She has lived in Europe, but now makes her home in Pennsylvania. She collects miniatures and holiday ornaments, tries to avoid exercise and has somehow found the time to write over twenty category romances.

One

"**M**r. Halford will see you now, Mr. McGrath." The smoothly polite tone of Miss Phyllis York, Arthur Halford's secretary, was perfunctory and correct, betraying not a hint of distaste or disapproval.

But Garrett McGrath did not rely solely on what he saw and heard. He had the instincts of a street fighter, acquired from growing up in a series of tough neighborhoods. Those instincts had proven to be an invaluable gift that had always served him well. And though he was no longer fighting in the streets, he'd adapted his instincts to his chosen trade, the hotel business. Sometimes the two had a lot in common.

He'd learned early that smiling faces too often masked hostility and contempt, and Garrett sensed both behind the proper Miss York's professional facade. Rather than resent it, Garrett admired the secretary's loyalty to her boss and to her place of employment—the exclusive, exalted, five-diamond, five-star resort, Halford House. He valued loyalty, however misplaced.

And he knew that to Miss York, a longtime Halford House employee, he was probably about as welcome as a degenerative disease. The name McGrath was anathema to Arthur Halford and his brethren at the high-end of the hotel industry, for the McGraths owned Family Fun Inns, a chain of budget motels at the lowest end of the scale. The premier hoteliers' usual policy of ignoring cheap motels for the masses had been severely challenged by Family Fun Inns, a wildly successful, recession-proof company that refused to be overlooked.

Family Fun Inns had a way of appearing in prime locations dominated exclusively by luxuriously elite resort hotels. The sight of the colorful motels, which resembled a crayon box with each door painted a different brilliant shade, inevitably evoked outraged squawks from high-end resort owners and their patrons. "A lethal weed choking the orchid" was the analogy the apoplectic Blue Springs Resort had issued when a Family Fun Inn joined them on their previously private island.

Garrett McGrath, chief weed, had built his career on encroaching among the orchids over and over again.

He'd worked hard in the beginning—eighteen-hour days, wheeling, dealing, planning, convincing, conniving—and his efforts had been very well rewarded. But lately, success had become too easy. Garrett recognized that he was bored, that he needed a challenge, something different.

Today was certainly providing it. Here he was, Garrett McGrath, commander in chief of the Family Fun Inns, being ushered into the plush executive office suite of the legendary Halford House, hallowed vacation spot of the rich and famous and those who were willing to pay the exorbitant fees to be near them.

His father would've loved it, thought Garrett. It amused him to speculate that perhaps the late Jack McGrath had a hand in it all from somewhere in the Great Beyond. The McGraths had a streak of mysticism mingled with a wicked humor, and this situation was rich in both. Garrett McGrath was here to buy Halford House, the very place that had refused to hire Jack and Kate McGrath as wait staff all those years ago because they weren't considered worthy enough to serve the exalted patrons.

And Garrett was savoring every minute of it.

Obviously Arthur Halford, one of the most urbane and patrician hoteliers in the business, was not. The older man's smile was decidedly forced and his expression became downright pained as he shook the hand that Garrett offered him. The steadfast Miss York hovered in the background, fixing Garrett with a look colder than ice.

"Today's the day, Art," Garrett said genially. "You have some papers ready for me to sign?"

"Mr. McGrath, I thought perhaps we would have lunch first, then meet with our attorneys for a final..." Arthur Halford paused and swallowed hard. "Perusal of the contract. Upon the—" this time he cleared his throat "—signing, I would like to invite you to join me in a celebratory glass of cognac."

Cognac. Garrett's eyes gleamed. He'd bet anything that Halford would rather serve him a shot of battery acid. Offering a celebratory drink of cognac was a nice touch. Classy. He'd have to keep that one in mind.

"I'd like to have lunch with you, Art, but do we really need the lawyers around? I didn't bring mine. Besides, they've already picked apart the deal word for word. My general counsel can recite the terms by heart. I assume there haven't been any changes since...." Garrett paused and stared hard at Arthur Halford.

The older man's face was flushed, his gaze darting frantically in an obvious attempt to avoid eye contact with Garrett. What a terrible poker player Halford must be, mused Garrett—the required blank poker face, giving away nothing, was clearly beyond him. Old Art had just given away everything, particularly himself. The vigilant Miss York looked alarmed.

"I'm going to take a wild guess and assume that there have been some changes," Garrett said flatly.

"Well, perhaps, but not exactly. Actually, y-you see—" stammered Halford.

"Don't try any whitewashing or stonewalling, just give me the cold, hard facts." Garrett's smile abruptly disappeared. He could be charming when he chose, but the hint of a double cross brought his fighting spirit to the fore. "What's going on, Halford?"

"*Mr.* Halford to you, Mr. McGrath," Miss York said imperiously, glowering at him like a dragon protecting the castle. "I'm mercifully unaware of the milieu in which you normally conduct your business, but here at Halford House we do *not* use first names, as if in the schoolroom, nor just last names, as if in a locker room. In the executive suite, we use the correct form of address and until this company changes hands—" she shuddered visibly at the thought "—we will continue to honor our traditions."

"Miss York, please," Halford said weakly. "It's all right." He looked bleakly at Garrett. "Mr. McGrath, I hope you will forgive my secretary for—"

"Forgive Miss York? I salute her! She's a dynamo. In fact, if you want to stay on here in your current position, Miss York, the job is yours." Garrett grinned, his good humor temporarily restored. Only Grandmother McGrath in her prime had ever dared to chew him out so effectively. A warm memory of the stone-faced old woman with the heart of granite suffused him. Good old Gran! He actually missed her sharp-tongued harangues, which had ceased since she'd decided to be fond of her eldest grandson.

"No, thank you." Miss York scowled, her disapproval unconcealed. "As soon as your team is in place, I'm retiring and that's final, Mr. McGrath."

"Too bad. I don't suppose you have a sister at home just like you? No?" Garrett shrugged. "Well, I hope you enjoy your retirement, Miss York. I'm sure it's well earned, and if you're ever in the vicinity of a Family Fun Inn, I want to offer you a discount to stay there as a personal friend of the McGrath family."

He reached into the pocket of his sport coat and pulled out one of his business cards to hand to her. "Just show them this. Discount guaranteed."

Miss York stared incredulously at the card.

"Miss York, if you'll excuse us, I have a personal matter to discuss with Mr. McGrath," Arthur Halford said in that cultured, well-modulated tone of his.

Miss York wordlessly withdrew. Garrett was heartened that she hadn't ripped his card to shreds and flung the pieces into the trash can. Instead, she'd tucked it into the pocket of her suit coat as she'd closed the office door behind her.

Garrett smiled. He'd bet this entire Halford House deal that Miss York would take him up on the discount and stay in a Family Fun Inn. And she'd like it, too, especially the oh-so-affordable prices. Another convert would be made. His grin broadened. There was nothing he liked better than winning, be it an argument, a court fight, a business deal, or merely changing someone's mind in his favor.

Which brought him back to this moment in time. It sounded ominously like Arthur Halford had changed *his* mind—but not in the McGraths' favor. Garrett narrowed his eyes, straightened his shoulders and assumed his take-charge, take-over, high-testosterone stance.

Nobody backed out on a deal with the McGraths. This was war. "I want to know what's suddenly gone sour with the deal, Art," he said with all the conviviality of a rattle-snake.

The suave and seasoned Arthur Halford seemed to dissolve in front of Garrett's very eyes. The older man sank down onto the forest green leather sofa, running a nervous hand through his thick silver hair. "My daughter!" he exclaimed miserably. "She's back! That's what's gone sour with the deal."

Garrett stared at him. "What does your daughter have to do with this? And where is she back from? Outer space? Prison?"

"California!" Halford practically wailed.

Garrett was genuinely nonplussed. "Excuse me, Art, but I don't get it. You're sitting here losing it because your daughter is back from California?"

"If you knew Shelby, you'd lose it, too," Halford intoned glumly. He was using vernacular he'd never used before, but somehow it fit. "And when she learns that I'm selling Halford House..." His voice trailed off, as if the consequences were too dire to voice.

Garrett was suddenly back on sure ground. "She's sentimental about the place, huh?" He sat down beside Halford. "Hey, let me talk to her. I have five younger sisters, I know something about explaining things to females. There might be a few tears but—"

"Tears? Ha! Shelby doesn't cry! I don't remember her ever crying, not even as an infant. She decides what she wants and she goes for it, and God help the person who tries to stand in her way. She has all the subtlety and tact of a nuclear missile." Arthur Halford shook his head. "She's as different from our Laney as a...a jackal is from a winsome little Yorkshire terrier. Laney has two, you know. Yorkies. She adores them." A fond, paternal smile momentarily brightened his face.

Garrett studied him curiously. He'd heard people compared to explosives—he'd even used the ticking-time-bomb reference himself—but he had never before heard a father describe his daughter as a jackal. In fact, as angry as Garrett had sometimes gotten at his younger sisters—and they could rile him plenty—he had never thought of them as jackals. Brats, maybe. Pests, perhaps. But nothing bestial.

He tried to get a mental picture of Shelby Halford but the only image that flashed to mind was one of snarling, sharp teeth and wild, beady eyes. Still, a deal was a deal, and he wanted the challenge and the prestige of adding a place like Halford House to the Family Fun Inn company. It would be the crown jewel in the rock-bottom budget chain, and he wasn't about to let some spoiled Halford brat ruin his plans. Even if she was a jackal.

Before he could speak, Arthur Halford rose to his feet and began to pace the floor of the office, clearly agitated. "Shelby has some hotel experience, you see. She majored in hotel management in college and has been working in California. For the past several years, our relationship has actually been quite excellent with us living on opposite sides of the country. But just last week she called to announce that she was moving back here to Florida."

"To work in the family business," Garrett concluded. "And you neglected to mention to her that you were selling Halford House."

"You've got it in one," said Halford gloomily. "You'll remember that we agreed to keep the deal secret until the papers were signed and the press release issued. I've told no one but my wife. So when Shelby called . . ." He shook his head and groaned. "Shelby has a way of dominating conversations. Before I could get a word in edgewise, she'd already told me she had quit her job, given up her apartment, and scheduled the movers. She gave me her date of arrival here in Port Key and told me she was ready to begin working here with me—as a prelude to taking over Halford House when I retire."

"And now she's here and you still haven't told her?"

Halford shook his head. "No, I still haven't told her. I . . . need more time. I have attempted to set the stage and ease into the subject, however."

"And how have you done that?" Garrett asked. Sophisticated, polished types like Halford interested him. He'd learned from experience that they were not pushovers, yet they did their back stabbing with such style. Garrett was the first to admit that he lacked deceptive subtlety; he was blunt, forceful and open. According to his mother, he'd been that way since he had first opened his eyes in the delivery room.

"I regret that my, er, explanation is a bit unorthodox." Arthur Halford appeared acutely embarrassed. "And so very, very difficult to explain, Mr. McGrath."

"This is going to be a good one," Garrett guessed, enjoying the anticipation. "Come on, Art. Spill it. What have you told Neutron Shelby about Halford House?"

"It's so wonderful to be home!" Shelby Halford exclaimed exuberantly, striding briskly through the lush gardens of the Halford House grounds. She nodded and smiled at some hotel guests who were enjoying a morning stroll along the meticulously maintained crushed gravel paths.

"Shelby, will you please slow down?" her younger sister Laney complained, half running to keep up with Shelby's long-legged stride. "The puppies are exhausted."

Shelby cast a disparaging eye at Laney's pair of five-year-old overfed, overweight Yorkshire terriers, who were panting from the exertion of their walk. "If they had more exercise and a lot less food, a short walk wouldn't wind them," she noted. "You simply have to put those dogs on a diet, Laney. It's for their own good. As it is, you're feeding them into an early grave."

"Stop it, Shelby!" Laney's velvety dark eyes filled with tears. "You can be so cruel—threatening my puppies with death when you know they mean the world to me." She turned to the tall, nattily dressed blond man who was walking slightly behind them. "Do you like animals, Paul?" she asked, dimpling prettily.

Paul gazed at her, seemingly mesmerized. His reaction surprised neither sister; people had been stopping dead in their tracks to stare at Laney Halford since she'd been a toddler. Paul had been gazing at her continuously since he'd arrived at Halford House last week.

Shelby viewed her sister more dispassionately. Laney was a classic beauty, a striking combination of Vivian Leigh in *Gone With the Wind* and Liz Taylor in *Ivanhoe*—except with enormous dark brown eyes. Everybody always said that Laney should be in movies, too, she was that beautiful. Laney always sweetly demurred; she didn't want a career in anything, she'd claim. All she ever wanted was to be a good wife and mother—Shelby was the one who wanted to work. The way Laney said it made people look askance at Shelby, as if she were against marriage and motherhood, and the American flag and apple pie, too.

Shelby sighed, remembering. There was so much she'd blocked out since leaving home for college in California ten years ago. But now she was back and everything was coming back to her. Every little thing.

"I've been an animal lover since I was a tiny little girl," Laney was saying to Paul, who was still gazing raptly at her. "I've always had a menagerie of dogs and cats and birds and bunnies, but Shelby's never had any time or interest in pets."

"You make it sound like I'm suffering from a personality disorder," Shelby said dryly. Laney was very good at that, she well knew.

"I suppose I'm just the maternal, nurturing type," Laney continued sweetly. "Shelby's the tough, competitive career woman in the family. And now she's back to help run Daddy's hotel. I'm so glad she brought you along to help her, Paul."

That seemed to snap Paul out of his Laney-induced stupor. "Halford House is as fabulous as you described it, Shelby," he said, his voice brimming with enthusiasm. "It's going to be a dream come true, working here."

He could have added "with you," Shelby thought wryly. But he might, given time, she told herself. She set her chin determinedly. *He would,* given time!

She and Paul Whitley had worked very well together at the regal Casa del Marina in California and their professional relationship had blossomed into a friendship that seemed poised on the brink of something deeper. When she had decided it was time to come home at last, she hadn't wanted to leave Paul behind, ending whatever hadn't even had a chance to begin. She'd invited him to join her at Halford House, careful to make no personal demands or expectations. There were no romantic strings tied to her job offer to Paul to become her second in command when she

succeeded her father. She had too much pride to attempt to
bribe a man into caring for her.

But she did have hopes. She'd always wanted marriage,
and motherhood, too, though she had never dared to admit
such dreams around Laney. Why couldn't she run Halford
House, be Paul's wife and their future children's mother—
and even have a dog, too? A healthy mongrel whose stomach wouldn't touch the ground when it walked.

"I guess Shelby told you that our cousin Hartley was being groomed to take over Halford House," Laney prattled
on to Paul, "but he was killed in a boating accident five
years ago. Poor Uncle Hal and Aunt Hillary—his parents—were so devastated, they sold their interest in the hotel to Daddy and moved to Arizona. I still cry for Hart. He
was a hero to me, a larger-than-life golden boy." She sniffed
delicately.

"God, that's so tragic," Paul gasped. He laid a consol-
ing hand on Laney's slim white arm. She gazed up at him
soulfully.

Shelby swallowed. She had fond memories of their cousin
Hart, too, but neither she nor Laney had ever been close to
him. Hart had been over a dozen years older and rarely
bothered to speak to either of them when he was around.
Laney's hero worship of her late cousin seemed to be a new
development. But it played well. As an attention getter, grief
was very effective, indeed. As Paul's tender efforts in trying to comfort her indicated.

"One of the reasons I came back was that I wanted Halford House to be run by a Halford," Shelby said heartily,
continuing the family saga. "Hart's brother Hal Junior isn't
interested in the hotel business and neither is Laney. So that
left me. And here we are."

"Here we are," Paul echoed, his eyes fixed on Laney.

"Just like old times, hmm, Shelby?" Lane said sweetly.

Shelby swallowed and straightened her shoulders. "Yes.
Just like old times."

A tanned, teenage bellboy, wearing the Halford House
uniform of white polo shirt and white slacks, approached

the trio, carefully stepping over the tubby little dogs. His name, Brad, was embroidered on the shirt pocket in dark green thread—the official color of Halford House known as "Halford green."

"Excuse me, Miss Halford," he addressed Shelby, though his eyes flicked admiringly over Laney. "I have a message from your father. He wants you to come to his office immediately. He said it's urgent."

Shelby nodded. "Thank you, Brad. I'll change clothes and go straight there."

"Mr. Halford said to come immediately," Brad insisted. "Like right this second. He said it was extremely urgent and not to waste any time getting over there."

Shelby looked down at her red running shorts and white cotton tank top. Running shoes and white socks completed the ensemble that was fine for her brisk walk through the gardens and subsequent run on the beach, but totally inappropriate for a business meeting in the hotel's executive office. Her hair was all wrong, too, pulled high into a ponytail instead of pinned tightly into her usual efficient chignon.

"You'd better go right away, Shelby," Laney advised. "You know how mad Daddy gets when you don't listen to him."

Shelby knew. Though she was loathe to appear in a business setting in sport attire, angering her father would be worse at this point. At least, it would be until he saw her in this getup, thus embarrassing him in front of his business associates. It was a typical Arthur and Shelby Halford no-win situation, variations of which they'd been playing for years. Everything she did seemed to upset her father, starting with being born a girl instead of the firstborn son he had so desperately wanted.

"I'll keep Paul company while you talk with Daddy, Shelby," Laney volunteered. "I'll give him another tour of the place and quiz him on it afterward." She smiled adorably, and both Paul and Brad looked ready to swoon.

"Thanks, Laney," Shelby said grimly. She had another flash from the old memory bank—Laney's penchant for enchanting any man in Shelby's orbit. It seemed Laney hadn't lost the knack. And Paul, that glazed-eyed satellite, was already spinning toward Laney's magnetic pull.

A few minutes later the door to Arthur Halford's office swung open and Shelby rushed in. Her father, staring out the wall of windows at the spectacular panoramic view of the sea, gasped and clutched his heart as he whirled around to face her. "Good heavens, young lady, you nearly startled the life out of me!"

Shelby's heart was pounding, too, her father's unexpected dramatic outburst having startled her just as violently. Now he was glowering furiously at her.

Defensive and embarrassed, Shelby struck back. "The bellboy, Brad, and three other people stopped me in the garden to tell me to get over here instantly. The minute I stepped in the door, Miss York demanded to know what had taken me so long to get here. You were expecting me, so how could I have startled you?"

"You have a point, but it's invalidated by your entrance, which was all wrong," came an amused voice from the other side of the office.

Shelby turned to face the direction of that voice. It belonged to a tall, muscular man lounging against the antique-papered wall. His sardonic grin lit a face of sharply carved features, including a pair of striking blue eyes, cool and assessing with a piercing intelligence and strangely at odds with his dark coloring. His hair was a thick black pelt that matched his eyebrows, which were currently arched high, giving him something of a satanic look. An arresting and very sexy look.

Shelby tried concentrating on his clothes instead. They were not terribly flattering, lacking all traces of expensive flair. His navy sport coat, white shirt and khaki slacks were reminiscent of a parochial school uniform and his striped tie was dull, totally lacking any pizzazz. In one of the exclusive men's shops in Halford House's charming shopping arcade were clothes off the rack with far more style and dash. And if a man preferred a custom-designed wardrobe, that was also available.

"Here at Halford House, one *always* knocks before entering," the man continued, his tone definitely mocking. Shelby detected an unacceptable trace of insolence in it, as well. "House rules, I believe. And while your offense is not punishable by death, it is a severe infraction that must be dealt with accordingly. Call the breach of etiquette police! Charges will be filed immediately."

He abruptly removed his boring navy sport coat and tossed it over the back of a chair, then began loosening the knot of his tie. His shoulders were broad and muscular beneath the crisp white material of his shirt, and he rolled the sleeves to his elbows, revealing strong forearms, covered with dark wiry hair.

Shelby's eyes widened. The man was shedding his clothes right in front of them! She wouldn't be surprised if he unfastened his belt buckle next. Thankfully, he didn't, but he continued to tug at his shirt, obviously uncomfortable with the stiff, starched material.

She watched him, unable to tear her eyes away. He emitted an intensity that struck her as demented and dangerous. Everything about him—his looks, his body language and mocking words—called forth an inner instinct urging her to turn and run from the office. It was the first time she'd ever had such a weird, primal reaction to anyone and she was completely shaken. It was as if she had some secret knowledge evoked from an unconscious level that was unavailable and inexplicable to her rational mind.

That irritated her. Anything that was unavailable and inexplicable to her rational mind was useless and unacceptable to her. Shelby prided herself on her analytical skills and keen grasp of logic, not to mention her firm grip on reality. Never once had she even mildly flirted with the New Age theories that had abounded during her ten-year stay in Southern California. The powers of crystals and channelers were not for her, nor were ridiculous primal instincts. Particularly when they involved this man, who was

watching her with an arrogant, amused air that both in-
sulted and infuriated her.

Shelby bristled. She would not serve as a source of
amusement to anyone! "Who are you?" she demanded
coldly.

Garrett did not enlighten her. "You have to be daughter
Shelby," he proclaimed instead.

He walked toward her, laughing, aware of the effort she
was exerting to remain still. He guessed how desperately she
wanted to back away from him but she stood rigidly in
place, not moving a muscle or even blinking as he came to
stand directly in front of her.

"You're not at all what I expected."

His eyes gleamed as they slowly slid over her, taking in
every inch of her from the top of her head to the athleti-
cally correct running shoes on her feet. It was absolutely
true, Shelby Halford was not the image of the militant bat-
tle-ax he'd conjured up from her father's descriptions.

Instead of the hatchet face he'd expected, hers was heart
shaped, with high cheekbones and full lips. And her lively,
alert hazel eyes had nothing in common with the beady-eyed
stare of a jackal. She had thick, straight, nut brown hair
pulled into a ponytail and a layer of bangs that accentuated
her big, wide-set eyes.

She was about five foot five, but seemed taller, probably
because of her impossibly long legs that seemed to reach all
the way to her armpits. Not that he had a single complaint
about that, Garrett admitted, studying the enticing curves
of her thighs, conveniently exposed for his scrutiny by her
bright red running shorts. And not even those clunky
sneakers of hers could disguise the fact that her calves were
slim and well shaped. He wondered if she ever wore four-
inch-high stiletto heels, but decided that this was not the
time to ask.

The rest of her body, slender and compact, was as pleasing as her legs. Softly flaring hips, narrow waist and firm,
rounded breasts now heaving with indignation against the
white cotton of her shirt. Garrett smiled, both intrigued and

satisfied. It seemed a whole new dimension had been added to his impromptu agreement to Halford's plea.

Shelby flushed at the intensity of his stare. She was not accustomed to blatant male once-overs. She took pride that her strict, no-nonsense air had always halted such sexist behavior.

He was so close she could feel the body heat emanating from him. At an inch or two over six feet, he seemed to tower over her, his frame solid and strong. She was not accustomed to such physicality—she needed her personal space. It took every ounce of willpower she possessed to keep herself locked in place, breathing in the scent of him.

He expected her to skittle away from him. In fact, she was certain he was counting on it. Well, she wasn't going to. If this was a battle of wills, Shelby intended to be the victor. "Stop leering at me!" she ordered, and was pleased she'd made it sound like an executive command.

"I'm not leering at you, I'm slavering over you," Garrett corrected. "*This* is leering." He leaned even closer, screwing his face into an insanely ridiculous grimace.

Shelby felt a wild, quick impulse to laugh and immediately stifled it. "I don't know whether you are trying to be funny or not, but I assure you that sexual harassment is not a laughing matter."

Arthur Halford groaned.

"Sexual harassment!" Garrett echoed with delight. "It's the issue of the '90s and this is my very first accusation. I'm in the loop at last! The family will be so proud."

Shelby swung away from him, her head held high. It didn't matter that she was the first one to move, she assured herself. It was time to end this stupid game of one-upmanship he'd begun and she was the one to do it. She was in charge here, not him.

"Dad, who is this...this person?" she demanded crossly. There were so many other nouns she would have rather used.

Garrett seemed to know it. He didn't bother to stifle his impulse to laugh.

Shelby knew he was laughing at her. She fumed.

Arthur Halford reddened, and he cast a worried, apologetic glance at Garrett.

"Please, introduce me to your charming daughter, Art," Garrett invited.

Two

Halford took a deep breath. "Mr. McGrath, I'd like to introduce you to my daughter, Shelby." He seemed to gulp for air. "Shelby, this is Garrett McGrath, the owner and CEO of the, uh, Family Fun Inns."

Shelby stared at him. "Garrett McGrath?" Now it was her turn to gasp. Everyone in the high-end of the hotel industry knew that name—some considered it interchangeable with Mephistopheles.

Garrett nodded his head. "Your father said he told you something about our arrangement, about why and how I've come here to Halford House to learn all about the upscale hotel business from my betters."

He glanced at Art. Poor Halford had cringed when he'd confessed the ruse he had cooked up to keep his daughter clueless regarding the sale. Garrett's first reaction had been incredulity, then his sense of humor had kicked in. He'd been more curious than ever to meet the demonic daughter who'd driven her father to such lengths. And now he'd met her.

Garrett's gaze slid over Shelby's lithe figure, then back to her sultry mouth and flashing hazel eyes. "This should be an interesting experience, to say the least."

"Interesting is hardly the word I'd choose," Shelby replied coldly. "The entire arrangement is ridiculous."

She was frustrated, exasperated. Didn't her father understand? Garrett McGrath was mocking them. That gleam in his impossibly blue eyes was derision, not friendly mirth. "And I told my father so. Having you stay here to observe the way we run Halford House is a complete waste of your time, Mr. McGrath." *And ours,* she added silently but implicitly.

Garrett arched his black brows higher. "Sounds like you're implying that nothing I learn here will be of any use to me in running Family Fun Inns."

"You know it won't," Shelby said tightly.

"I assume rich people have families and want to have fun, just like the patrons of the Family Fun Inns. So isn't it possible that—"

"You're deliberately goading me, Mr. McGrath," Shelby cut in. "And I—"

"I'm just trying to learn from you, Your Highness." It was Garrett's turn to interrupt and he did so, grinning broadly. "So far, I haven't learned much about running a swank joint like Halford House but I've learned that when you're on the losing side of an argument, you take the offensive. Accusing me of goading you is a good diversionary tactic, although it didn't work. You still haven't convinced me why I shouldn't be here to learn about serving the high and mighty."

Shelby's mouth tightened. "Are you always so argumentative, Mr. McGrath?"

"Always," he assured her. "Usually, I'm even worse, but I'm on my best behavior today. I'm hoping to impress my superiors here at Halford House. How am I doing?"

Her father didn't give her a chance to reply. "Please don't take offense at anything Shelby says, Mr. McGrath. She's wary of new acquaintances and . . . um . . . tries to test them.

As for me, I'm happy and proud to share my forty-some years' knowledge of the business with a man as brilliant and innovative as you.''

Shelby stared at her father as if he'd taken leave of his senses. "Dad, may I remind you that this is the Garrett McGrath who put a Family Fun Inn on the same island as the Blue Springs Resort, sending their property value and stock into a free-fall. Who built a Family Fun Inn practically next door to the Snow Bird Hacienda in Aspen and caused its patrons to flee the state. Whose Family Fun Inns and their faithful retinue of T-shirt shops, themed burger joints, frozen yogurt stands and souvenir junk places have taken over formerly quaint little towns and turned them into tourist traps. I can recite the names of them, beginning with—''

"Stop, you're embarrassing me!" Garrett's blue eyes taunted her. "There's no need to tout the spectacular success of Family Fun Inns. Just basking in the glow of your admiration is praise enough.''

"I do not admire you and I'm certainly not praising you!'' cried Shelby.

"You take the bait every time, don't you, honey?'' Garrett surveyed her lazily. "Oh, yes, working here with you the next couple of months is definitely going to be interesting.''

"Couple of months?'' both Shelby and her father chorused in pure dismay.

"Why not?'' Garrett shrugged. "I haven't taken a vacation in ages. Of course, I stay at Family Fun Inns all over the country throughout the year, but that's work, not a vacation. So I think I'll take one here. Sort of a busman's holiday, if you will. A high-end one.''

Shelby felt a peculiar panic ripple through her, growing stronger the more she contemplated the prospect of a steady daily diet of Garrett McGrath. "You can't stay here, Mr. McGrath,'' she blurted out.

"Shelby!'' There was nothing well modulated or polished in the roar that Arthur Halford emitted as he glared at his daughter. "Mr. McGrath is our guest. Our honored guest. He is welcome here as long as he cares to stay."

The smile Garrett flashed at Shelby set her teeth on edge. "Thanks, Art. I'll take that cottage you so graciously offered me earlier and settle in. Of course, I'll be flying home to our corporate headquarters in Buffalo for a day or so every week to stay in touch, but with faxes and teleconferences, I'll be able to manage things very well from down here."

"Your corporate headquarters are in Buffalo?" Halford repeated with forced joviality. "I hadn't realized that."

"The first Family Fun Inn was in Niagara Falls," Garrett explained. "My family had ended up in Buffalo, after living in a string of cities. We were sort of like Gypsies, traveling from place to place."

"That certainly fits," muttered Shelby. She could easily visualize caravans of McGraths descending on one world-class resort after another, fleecing them of their worth.

Her father shot her a quelling glance, then turned to Garrett. "Well, we're delighted you are here at Halford House, Mr. McGrath." Halford was once again the quintessential host welcoming his guest. "September is an ideal time to learn the ropes of running, um, a place like this. Our peak season is in winter and early spring when freezing weather up north brings our guests here to Port Key for some sun and warmth."

"Summer is peak season for Family Fun Inns," Garrett said, "although we do well during school holidays, especially Christmas break. Our inns are swarming with kids during school vacations." He smiled. "Speaking as the oldest of nine, I think kids are great. There can never be too many of them around. What are your facilities for children here at Halford House?"

Shelby and her father exchanged uneasy glances. When he hesitated to reply, she stepped in to tackle the question. "We don't get very many children here," she admitted. She felt as if she'd been called to the principal's office, condemned by a failing grade. "Many of our guests are older," she hastened to explain. "Their children are grown, with families of their own. We do have a wonderful children's boutique in our arcade of shops that is filled with unique gifts for doting grandparents to buy. It does very well," she added lamely.

"I've seen some of the guests around here and they aren't all grandparents," Garrett challenged. "There are younger people staying here."

"We have many childless, two-income couples who like to come here to relax." Shelby wondered why she felt so defensive and was irked that she did. "Then, of course, there are the couples who do have young children but who come here to be alone."

"Leaving the kids behind," Garrett said flatly.

"Where is it written that parents can't take a vacation without their children?" Shelby flared.

"Shelby, you're talking to a man who has built a chain of motels dedicated to the proposition of parents vacationing with their children," her father reminded her. "We sincerely respect your position, Mr. McGrath, and we admire your incredible success," he added with a fulsome smile.

Her father sounded like a fawning sycophant! Shelby gaped at him. Could this be the same man who'd always expounded at length on the horrors of having to cater to guests under twelve? Who'd considered banning teenagers from the premises—unless they were working here at less than minimum wage. It was safe to say that Arthur Halford did not dote on children. Shelby could personally attest to that, having grown up as one of his own.

Garrett glanced at his watch. "I have some calls to make," he announced abruptly. He grabbed his sport coat and headed toward the door.

"Shelby will escort you to your cottage," Halford offered at once. "And she will be at your disposal until we meet for lunch at one. I have a table reserved on the terrace—if that meets with your approval?" He glanced deferentially at Garrett.

"Lunch on the terrace at one sounds good to me," affirmed Garrett.

It didn't sound good to Shelby. It was just ten o'clock, which meant that she was doomed to spend three whole hours with the insufferable Garrett McGrath before passing him along to her father. She couldn't do it, Shelby decided.

She turned to her father. "Dad, as you know, you gave me this morning off and I've already made plans. I can't possibly—"

"Change your plans," her father ordered, glaring balefully at her. "In case you've forgotten, I am still the one to give orders around here and I am ordering you to devote yourself to Mr. McGrath's service."

He turned to Garrett, all smiles once more. "You'll be staying in cottage 101," he added, naming one of the largest, most elegant and newly refurbished cottages on the grounds. Like the rooms and suites in Halford House's main lodge, the outlying cottages comprising the complex had the full range of hotel services.

"I'm sure you'll feel quite at home there, Mr. McGrath," Halford continued expansively. "Presidents and royalty have stayed in 101 and been very pleased with the facilities."

"Presidents, royalty, and now a McGrath," Garrett remarked as they left the office, Shelby trailing slightly behind him. He seemed to be laughing at his own private joke.

And the joke was on her, Shelby was certain of that. They passed Miss York's desk and Garrett bade her a cheerful goodbye. Unsmiling, the secretary acknowledged him with a grim nod.

"At least Miss York is still in character," Shelby muttered as they approached the main desk in the main lobby.

"According to your father's description, so are you."

Shelby asked for and received the keys to cottage 101, then strode briskly from the building into the bright Florida sunshine. She knew Garrett was ambling behind her and she paused to wait for him by a tall palm tree. She had to ask, she couldn't put it off another minute. "What did my father say about me?" she demanded.

"That you've just returned from a ten-year stay in California among other things." Garrett faced her squarely.

"And those other things are?"

He shrugged. Though it might surprise those who had previously accused him of heartlessness and lack of tact, he wasn't about to tell her that her own father considered her as feral as a jackal. "He mentioned that you're different from your sister Lacey, or Lynnie, or something like that."

"Laney," Shelby corrected. She was appalled that her father had been discussing her with this man. And if he'd been comparing her to Laney, she could well imagine which sister had fared the worst. "Her name is Maclane but she's always been Laney."

"Shelby and Maclane. Sounds like a law firm."

"Garrett McGrath. Sounds like an aspiring country music singer."

"Merely an *aspiring* singer?" Garrett complained mildly. "How about a country-music legend instead?"

Shelby shook her head. "An aspiring singer. One who never even gets to make a demo tape and ends up as a dishwasher at a Nashville diner."

"Ouch! Okay, then Shelby and Maclane are a pair of disreputable ambulance chasers rather than a staid, established firm."

Shelby scowled at him. "This is the most ridiculous conversation I've ever had."

"Really?" Garrett shrugged. "It's fairly typical for me."

"Why doesn't that surprise me?" She glanced at him curiously. "Are you really the oldest of nine?"

"Sure am. In descending order—Glenn, Gracie, Fiona, Eilish, Devon, Caitlin, Brendan and Aidan. Are there just you and your sister Laney?"

"Just the two of us. She's fourteen months younger than me," Shelby said flatly.

"And she loves cute little dogs. You, on the other hand, eat them for breakfast. Metaphorically speaking, of course."

Shelby groaned. "What else did my father tell you about me?"

"It wasn't so much what he said as the way he said it. I admit that I don't know the man very well, but from what I've seen so far, Arthur Halford is a first-rate hotelier, but definitely loses in the father sweepstakes."

Shelby's temper, too close to the surface around Garrett McGrath, flared once again. "I can't believe you have the gall to criticize my father after he's offered you the hospitality of Halford House and agreed to allow you a kind of on-the-job training in its operations."

"He's something of a dud as a dad, but you defend him," Garrett observed. "You're a very loyal daughter. Is that why you came back from California, Shelby? For the opportunity to work side by side with your father and—"

"Why do you ask?" she cut in sharply.

"I'm curious as to why you decided to return to Port Key and Halford House after living so far away for ten years. Your father claimed he didn't know the reason, either, that you suddenly announced you were on your way back here."

"My reasons for returning are personal and none of your business, Mr. McGrath," Shelby said stiffly. She turned away from him, taking a path into the lush tropical gardens.

"If you make it a mystery, you'll only encourage me not to give up until I know everything," warned Garrett, right at her heels. "There's nothing I like better than a challenge."

"And all along I thought your favorite thing was slapping up dirt-cheap motels where they aren't wanted."

"It's not the dirt-cheap motels snobs like you object to, it's the people who stay in them. You don't want working-class people, the lower and middle classes, anywhere around you." Garrett moved closer and caught her wrist, bringing her to an abrupt halt. His blue eyes were glittering. "We do get some upper middle-class folks who want a good bargain and don't care about status, but status and flashing big bucks are all you spoiled little rich girls and your cohorts care about. That and the thrill of excluding everyone who doesn't meet with your rigid class standards of approval."

"I'm not a snob!" Shelby protested. "And I'm certainly not spoiled. My parents paid for my education but they never showered me with presents or made me feel like I was better than anyone else."

On the contrary, she usually felt she wasn't as good. She flinched at the painful insight and pushed it away to resume her defense. "I'm twenty-seven years old and I've had to work hard to achieve everything I've accomplished from..." Her voice trailed off. "I don't have to defend myself to you."

"True," agreed Garrett. "Although you seem to feel the need, don't you?"

He had a point and she could think of no suitable reply. After all, why should she care what Garrett McGrath thought of her? If he wanted to believe she was an elitist snob, it shouldn't matter to her at all.

His hand was still clamped around her wrist and Shelby jerked it free. She didn't say another word as she led him through the gardens to the secluded grove where cottage 101 was artfully landscaped with an assortment of riotously colored flowers, bushes and shrubs. "Here's the cottage, here's your key." She shoved it into his hand. "Goodbye, Mr. McGrath."

"Not goodbye," he countered. "According to your dear old dad's explicit orders, you're supposed to be at my disposal until I meet him for lunch."

Shelby took a deep breath. "Mr. McGrath, you don't like me any more than I like you. We're incompatible, and you can't possibly want to prolong the misery. Besides, you have phone calls to make. You said so in my father's office."

"I lied," Garrett said bluntly. "I was getting bored listening to your father sucking up to me. And call me Garrett, because I refuse to call you Miss Halford, even though

Miss York read me the riot act on proper terms of address here at Halford House.''

He inserted the key into the lock and pushed open the door. ''And who says I don't like you? I'm quite selective in choosing my enemies and I don't know you well enough to consider you one.'' He stepped inside the cottage. ''Come on in,'' he ordered, motioning her to follow him.

Shelby stood in the doorway and watched him prowl around the room like a restless tiger moving in on new territory. The living room was spacious and luxurious, a sunny, airy room with white wicker furniture, the color scheme Halford green and complementing shades of yellow and peach.

Garrett disappeared down a small hallway that Shelby knew led to the kitchen, bathroom and bedroom. Another turn to the right led to the larger master bedroom suite. Her mouth felt oddly dry and she remained in the doorway, her fists clenched tightly at her sides.

''Help yourself to something in the refrigerator, I'm sure it's fully stocked,'' Garrett called from the back of the cottage. ''And close the door. You're air-conditioning the state of Florida and wasting electricity.''

Leave, Shelby advised herself. Turn around and march out right now. She almost did it. But instead she stepped inside, closing the door behind her. She really had no choice. Garrett McGrath was unpredictable; he might simply go about his business after she'd left or he might call her father and report her defection.

And her father was a man capable of great wrath when things were not to his liking. Shelby was quite aware of that because much of what she did was not to his liking. But could pleasing Garrett McGrath possibly be to his liking? Shelby sat gingerly on the edge of the flowered chintz sofa and pondered that astonishing concept. Why was her father trying to ingratiate himself with Garrett McGrath?

She couldn't buy her father's fulsome declarations of respect and admiration for the man. Though she'd been living away from Arthur Halford since the age of seventeen, they'd maintained telephone contact and the occasional visit. She still knew her father well enough to know that he considered low-end, fast money-makers like Garrett McGrath the bane of the hotel industry.

"Ready?"

She was lost in thought and gave a startled gasp at the sound of Garrett's voice. He was standing beside the arm of the sofa, towering above her. Shelby jumped to her feet and moved a safe distance away from him. He had changed into dark blue running shorts and a white cotton tank top similar to her own.

Shelby stole a sidelong, furtive glance at him. His legs were long and muscular and covered with dark, wiry hair. The tight shirt showcased his broad chest and shoulders and his hard, muscled arms. Her gaze slid up to his face, taking in his strong jaw and disturbingly sensuous mouth. Their eyes met, and for one long moment Shelby gazed into their dark, deep blue depths. She felt the frisson of sensual electricity surge between them and immediately turned away.

"You're going to work out? We have an excellent exercise spa, all sorts of state-of-the-art workout equipment, a sauna, and a masseur." She paused to breathe. She couldn't seem to stop talking. "We also boast a fully—"

"I'm going to run on the beach. And since you're under paternal command to stick to me like superglue, so are you."

Shelby heaved a martyred sigh.

Garrett laughed. "Don't even try to pretend this is some big sacrifice for you. You were on your way to run when your daddy summoned you to his royal headquarters."

"How do you know what I was going to do?" Shelby challenged. "Are you now claiming to be psychic?"

"Just observant. I can tell by the way you're dressed. You seem like the type who would make a point of dressing correctly for whatever you're doing and wherever you're going. So if you were going to play tennis, you'd be wearing tennis whites. If you were going to the exercise spa, you'd

be in a bright spandex leotard and tights. If you were golf-
ing, you'd—"

"All right, I get your point! I was planning to run on the
beach," she admitted crossly. "I try to run every morning,
although this is later than usual for me."

"Because your father gave you the morning off," concluded Garrett. "Until he rescinded it and stuck you with
me."

Shelby shot him an exasperated glance. "Precisely."

They jogged in silence along the wide white span of sandy
beach, side by side, keeping a steady pace. There were a few
bathers sunning themselves on Halford House canvas beach
chairs. A lifeguard was on duty in a wooden kiosk but there
were no swimmers in the ocean.

"I can tell you run every day," Garrett said at last.

"How?" Shelby asked dryly. "By my impeccably correct attire?" She was sorry to break the silence that had
grown almost companionable as they headed around a
curve, out of sight of the Halford House facilities. A long
expanse of deserted beach stretched before them.

"You're not winded and you're doing a nice job of keeping up with me," stated Garrett.

"That's funny, I was about to say the same thing about
you."

"I wasn't patronizing you, I meant it as a compliment."

Shelby gave him a saccharine smile. "Now why would I
ever think otherwise?"

They lapsed into silence once more, jogging farther along
the uninhabited beach. The only sounds to be heard were
those of the surf breaking and the gulls crying. It was
peaceful and quiet, and Shelby felt the tension begin to
slowly drain from her, the exercise working its loosening
magic.

"So, are you going to tell me what prompted your sudden return to Halford House?" Garrett's voice shattered the
peace.

Shelby tensed again. "I will if you'll tell me why my father seems to have suddenly become your number one fan."

Garrett grinned. "Suspicious about that, are you?"

"I'm not as stupid or gullible as you may think, Mr. McGrath."

"Garrett," he corrected. "And I don't think you're stupid or gullible at all. Quite the contrary." He stopped running, and because she was at his disposal, Shelby stopped, too.

"I want to cool off. Let's go swimming." Garrett stooped to untie his running shoes.

"In the ocean?"

He looked up at her. "Where else?"

Shelby bit back a smile. It had been a stupid question, what with the ocean just a foot away. "I'm not going into the water."

"Because you aren't properly dressed for the proposed activity," Garrett surmised. "I'm going to tell you something shocking, Shelby. You don't have to wear a swimsuit to go into the water."

"If you're talking about taking an uninhibited skinny-dip in the ocean, forget it. I won't do it. And don't bother pointing out that my father has placed me at your services. My services do not include—"

"You're awfully bossy," Garrett complained. He'd already removed his own shoes and socks and had started to untie the laces of her shoes. He was close enough for his shoulder to brush her leg as he worked. Shelby gulped. The feel of his skin against hers and the scent of his clean male sweat evoked a sharp, hot pang deep within her.

Shelby closed her eyes and took a deep breath. She would not, *could* not, be attracted to this man. What she was experiencing was not sexual excitement but ragged nerves, caused by apprehension and anxiety and lack of breakfast, she assured herself.

When he tried to take off her shoe, she resisted the impulse to kick him and moved swiftly out of his reach. "So, I'm sure a staunch advocate of family fun like you must have a wife and children—stashed away in Buffalo, perhaps? And what will they think of your months' long vacation away from them? Unless, of course, you intend to bring them to Halford House to join you in the cottage?''

Garrett rose to his feet. "Ah, the inevitable question. Am I married or not? That was a less than subtle approach, Shelby.''

"I wasn't trying to be subtle." Her cheeks were fiery red. "And I don't care whether you are or you aren't.''

"I see. You simply wanted to know how many towels to supply to the cottage. Well, I've never been married and I don't have kids. Hmm, how can I make this more interesting ... ?" He paused. "I've got it. Thirty-six-year-old, single, white male likes frozen yogurt, burger joints and T-shirt shops—''

"Cheap souvenirs, taffy and fudge shops and family fun," Shelby added. "Don't forget to mention how you love to sit in front of a roaring fire, listen to rain on the roof and go for long walks on the beach.''

"I run on the beach, I get too hot sitting in front of a roaring fire, and the sound of rain annoys me. It means a ruined vacation. I prefer sun or snow, seasonable weather in seasonable places.''

They looked at each other and laughed. Their gazes locked and lasted after their laughter faded, crossing the intangible line into sensual awareness. Garrett's breath caught in his throat. Shelby's eyes were shining, her mouth wide and soft and tempting. His blood seemed to thicken and surge hotly through him, pooling in one hard throbbing strategic area. Now he *needed* the shock of a cold water plunge.

Shelby felt the sexual tension stretch between them. Her pulse accelerated and her breathing quickened. She quickly looked away from him.

"So, now that you know I'm a wholesome, honorable, single guy instead of a married cad bent on cheating on his wife, will you go swimming with me?" Garrett said huskily. "With our clothes on.''

"Just run right into the ocean wearing our clothes?"

"Well, you made it pretty clear that you weren't interested in skinny-dipping."

Shelby hesitated. It occurred to her that she had never swum wearing anything but the appropriate attire, a swimsuit. During staff parties at Casa del Marina, managers and senior staff were sometimes rowdily tossed into the pool, fully dressed, by some exuberant revelers. Not Shelby, though. She'd never even been approached. She was not the type to inspire anyone, not even a wildly exuberant reveler, to pick her up and throw her into the water.

"You have no choice, you know." Garrett's voice sounded above her head. "I'll give you thirty seconds to take off your shoes and socks and then I'm dragging you into the water, with or without them."

Without saying a word, Shelby pulled off her socks and shoes and tossed them aside. "I'll race you into the water," she called over her shoulder as she sped into the waves.

It was an unfair contest as she was already on her way before she issued the challenge, but Garrett responded at once. He ran into the surf, water splashing high around him.

"I win," sang Shelby, standing knee-deep in the water. It was lukewarm and felt refreshing against her overheated skin.

"You cheated," Garrett countered.

"Don't be a sore loser. After all, it's not whether you win or lose, it's if you play the game."

"*How* you play the game," amended Garrett.

"Whatever." Shelby shrugged. "There aren't any waves today. The ocean is as still and clear as a swimming pool. Which is where you should be, if you wanted to swim today," she added, casting him a reprimanding glance.

"But you can't do this in a pool." Suddenly, without a hint of a warning, Garrett placed his hands around Shelby's waist.

Shelby felt heat flare within her. Their eyes met and held and a heavy silence engulfed them. Was he going to kiss her? she wondered. Did she want him to? Her heart was thundering madly against her ribs so hard and so loud, the beats echoed in her ears.

As she was pondering those questions, she felt his strong fingers tighten around her waist, felt him lifting her up, up off her feet. A dizzying, disorienting moment later, she was flying through the air and then plunging back into the water several feet away from him. She went under and came up spluttering.

Shelby grabbed a handful of her wet hair and pushed it out of her eyes. "You threw me!" she gasped.

"You've got a keen grasp of the obvious."

Shelly waded through the water, which lapped around her waist, back to where Garrett stood. He was grinning down at her, unrepentantly.

She found herself grinning back. "It was fun. Do it again."

Three

———

Garrett obliged. He picked her up by her waist, raised her out of the water and tossed her as easily as a beach ball. Once again, Shelby experienced the rush of sailing through the air and crashing back into the warm, clear water. Once again, she waded back to him.

"Again?" he asked.

She nodded. He picked her up and threw her again. Shelby emerged from under the water, laughing.

"One more time?" suggested Garrett.

He didn't wait for her reply but waded over to her, picked her up and tossed her back into the ocean. "Now it's your turn to throw me," he said when Shelby surfaced.

She eyed his solid, hard frame. "You've got to be kidding."

"Come on," he urged. "You at least have to try."

"What do you think I am? A sumo wrestler? I can't pick you up!"

"You can in the water. It negates gravity or something."

"'Negates gravity'?" Shelby repeated scornfully. "I'll bet you were a whiz in physics class with theories like that."

"I never took physics," Garrett confessed. He cupped his hand and splashed a spray of water at her. "I wasn't into science. My talents lay elsewhere—like in the cheap-motel industry."

"And in unassailable concepts like family fun," Shelby added. She vigorously splashed him back. "Personally, I've always considered family fun to be an oxymoron. You know, a complete contradiction in terms."

"Having met your father, I can understand why. Are your mother and sister as bad or worse?"

Shelby used both hands to shower him with blasts of water. "My mother is a dear. Everybody loves her. My sister is..." Her voice trailed off. How to describe Laney?

Garrett drew his own conclusions. "A jackal?" he suggested.

She shouldn't have laughed, Shelby scolded herself after she'd already done so. She tried to repair the damage. "Wait until you see Laney. You'll be tripping over your tongue as you spout accolades to her beauty."

"I never spout accolades," Garrett assured her.

He glided swiftly through the water to stand before her. "Are you going to toss me or not?" he challenged.

"I told you, it's impossible. Look." Shelby tentatively placed her hands on his waist. Her fingers locked around his wet skin, she felt his hard warmth beneath her palms. "See, I can't budge you. You're solid as a...a..." The husky thickness of her voice surprised her, and she lost her train of thought.

Her eyes flew to his face, just as he lowered his head to hers. Before she had a chance to speak or move or even think, Garrett's arms came around her and his mouth took hers.

For a split second Shelby was so startled she stood rigid in his embrace, her eyes wide open, her lips closed. She was pressed so tightly against him that she could feel him everywhere, enveloping her in his seductive masculine heat. She was achingly aware of the virile, burgeoning strength of him throbbing against her, of the muscular hardness of his chest crushing her breasts.

His mouth was seductively firm and tasted of saltwater, his big hands moved slowly and sensuously over her, molding her ever closer against the taut male planes of his body. Shelby's eyelids drifted shut as her arms crept around his neck. Her mind seemed to have short-circuited, giving her body free reign to do as it liked. And it most definitely liked these exciting, enthralling feelings coursing through her. A glowing warmth flamed deep in her belly, and she felt a secret intimate ache that swelled and throbbed within her.

Her lips parted for him and his tongue penetrated the warm wetness of her mouth, deepening the kiss. Shelby moaned when his tongue rubbed hers, stroking in tantalizing sensual simulation.

He slipped his thigh between hers and she yielded to him, parting her legs to accommodate the thrusting male pressure. Hot, sweet pleasure streaked through her. Shelby clung to him, drowning in a smooth silky sea of desire. As if of their own volition, her hands moved over the taut muscles of his back, reveling in the solid masculine feel of him. Her fingers dared to move lower, to the strong muscular curve of his buttocks.

Garrett lifted his mouth from hers and, groaning, buried his lips in the soft, damp curve of her neck. He was breathing hard and his heartbeat was hammering in his ears, as if he'd been running in a high-speed race. He clutched her possessively, caressing her, inhaling her sweet and salty scent.

The feel of her soft hands on him was so arousing that his mind seemed to splinter. When she uttered a small, sexy moan, he took her mouth again. He tilted her head back, slanting his mouth more securely over hers to deepen the kiss and heighten the intimacy.

Shelby kissed him back with an ardor and a passion she had never before experienced. Her senses seemed to be excruciatingly attuned to him, to their kiss and her own wild responses. Her breasts were pressed against the wall of his chest, and their sensitive tips tightened with aching pleasure. Shelby twisted feverishly against him, rising on tiptoe to fit herself even more intimately into him. A syrupy warmth flowed through her. His mouth was hot and hard and demanding, and she loved it.

They kissed hungrily, fiercely, their kisses growing wilder and hotter and longer, one blending into another. Garrett's hands were in constant motion, touching her all over, caressing the curve of her breasts, her waist and hips. Cupping the rounded firmness of her bottom, his long fingers kneaded through the wet cotton covering her. He longed to strip it off, to see her, to feel her without the restricting material. He stroked the backs of her thighs, up and down in a sensually mesmerizing rhythm, then slipped his fingers under the wide-cut hem of her shorts.

Shelby felt his fingertips trace the elastic leg band of her panties, then slip audaciously underneath. The intimacy was shocking enough to jar her sense of time and of place back to the fore. Abruptly, she jerked herself away from him, her withdrawal so quick and unexpected that Garrett had no time to prevent her.

And he definitely would have prevented her from pulling out of his arms, he admitted, as he stared dazedly down at her. She was looking at him, her lips moist and slightly swollen from their kisses, her hazel eyes cloudy with passion. A shudder of desire racked him. He wanted nothing more than to yank her back into his arms and kiss her until they were both senseless.

And Shelby knew it. The intensity in his blue gaze made her quiver. "I—it's broad daylight and we're right here in the ocean," she murmured shakily. "Anyone walking along the beach could see us...." Her voice trailed off. She was shaken and off-balance by her wild uninhibited response to him, and more than a little unnerved by the completeness of her surrender.

Garrett's mouth curved into a slow, sexy smile. "Do you want to go back to the cottage and continue this there?"

"No!" Shelby exclaimed, horrified. She had regained full control of herself. The unbridled passion that had sparked between them only moments ago now seemed impossible and inconceivably out of character for her. One moment they had been playing and splashing in the water together and the next they'd been locked in a hot embrace.

Shelby frowned. When was the last time she'd played and splashed in the water? When she'd been three? Perhaps four? Certainly by the time she had reached kindergarten age, she had learned to take swimming seriously and had abandoned all water play.

"Are you sure?" Garrett reached out his arm to run his thumb along the length of her bare arm. Shelby jumped away from him, as if he'd burned her with a match, the pathway of skin he'd traced, hot and tingling.

"I'm positive!" she snapped. "I—I don't even like you!"

"You don't, hmm?" Garrett arched his brows. "You could've fooled me, honey."

A hot bolt of anger streaked through her. "Don't call me honey! I'm not one of your floozies!"

"Floozies?" Garrett laughed out loud. "Where did you come up with that one? Masterpiece Theater?"

Shelby glared at him. "I suppose this is standard operating procedure for you—your obligatory pass at the boss's daughter. But let me tell you it's disgusting and demeaning. Do you need to...to validate your masculinity by making a pass at every woman you meet?"

"Your father is not my boss," Garrett said calmly. "And I had no doubts about my masculinity, although if I had, your passionate response certainly would've...um... validated it."

He moved closer, close enough to trace the taut outline of her nipple, which was defined and straining against the double layers of wet cloth plastered to her. He touched the pad of his thumb to the tight center and rubbed gently.

Shelby gasped as fiery sparks of pleasure flared and burned deep in the most secret part of her. She immediately slapped his hand away, as enraged by his unspeakable boldness as by her own traitorous response to it.

"I'm leaving," she announced, turning to the shore. "I refuse to spend another moment in your company. You can entertain yourself until your lunch with my father."

"Shelby," he called.

Shelby didn't stop walking, though she looked over her shoulder to glower imperiously at him. "If you try to stop me, I'll fight you," she promised. "I took a self-defense class and I can do major damage."

"I'm letting you go," Garrett called back, "because I want to, not because I'm even remotely worried about your fighting ability."

He watched her wade out of the water and storm up the beach to snatch her shoes and socks. She didn't bother to put them on, but broke into a run along the sand in the direction of the hotel.

Garrett stayed in the water, watching her until she disappeared from view. He wasn't as cool as he'd led her to believe. He was thoroughly flummoxed by his incendiary response to her. He had kissed her on impulse, but he'd never expected her passionate response, which, in turn, had sent him soaring into the sexual stratosphere.

There was something downright fateful about the whole thing. His Grandmother McGrath was big on fate, always seeing its determining hand in everything, Garrett recalled with a smile. He was more prosaic and pragmatic himself. What Gran called fate, he called timing. The timing had to be right in buying and selling, just as timing was everything in sex, love and friendship.

Right now, the timing seemed highly auspicious. His first venture into the high-end hotel business had led to an encounter with a woman who interested, amused and aroused him.

He didn't take it lightly. The motel business was Garrett's real love and he'd come to accept that. He never expected to meet a woman as compelling to him as his business dealings.

Not that he had much opportunity to look for one. was simply too busy to spend much time on his social life. There were too many other demands on his time. Since business took him all over the country, he was never in one place long enough to cultivate a serious relationship, though he'd had a certain number of no-strings, temporary ones. What red-blooded single man who'd reached the age of thirty-six hadn't?

Lost in thought, Garrett slowly retraced his path to the hotel. Timing, he thought again. For the past year he'd been growing tired of the way things were and had finally decided to halt his descent into boredom and make some changes in his life. Adding the Halford House to the Family Fun Inns had been a professional change but it seemed that it might be time to make other changes, as well. Changes involving his personal life and those no-strings, temporary relationships.

Would Shelby Halford be part of those changes or was she merely the catalyst for what was to come? He didn't know the answer but the question intrigued him.

Halford House's formal dining room overlooked the ocean, providing a spectacular view for the diners. A smaller, more casual dining room known as The Grill was centrally located in the complex, surrounded by two huge, crystal blue pools, complete with cascading waterfall and poolside bar. Also on the premises were tennis courts, a golf course and a spa, all equipped with their own staff. A dock and marina adjacent to the private beach made sailboats, Jet Skis and catamarans available for hourly or daily rentals. The arcade of exclusive shops and the nightclub with live entertainment and dancing provided diversions for those guests uninterested in land or water sports.

"I'm impressed," Garrett said as he toured the facilities with Shelby, pretending that it was the first time he'd seen them.

"It's like a world unto itself," Paul Whitley enthused. "A perfect world. Only the very best for the very best people."

Garrett glared at him. When Arthur Halford had instructed Shelby to give Garrett a detailed, guided tour of the
facilities this afternoon, he hadn't mentioned that this
bronze, blond surfer in the ice-cream suit would be part of
the group.

Only the very best for the very best people. Whitley's
elitist sentiment instantly grated on Garrett. He visualized
a 1940s version of Paul Whitley informing young Jack and
Kate McGrath that they couldn't be hired to serve the re-
vered patrons of Halford House because they didn't qualify, classwise. *Only the very best for the very best people.*

"Exactly what is your function here, Whitley?" Garrett
asked, and received an icy look of disapproval from Shelby
for his slightly challenging tone. But he was genuinely puz-
zled. Arthur Halford had made no mention of Paul Whitley, though he seemed to have some sort of official function
around here. And some sort of connection to Shelby. Garrett frowned.

"Paul was the evening assistant manager at the Casa del
Marina Resort in California," Shelby replied before Paul
had a chance to. "He was highly thought of there, and we
here at Halford House are very fortunate that he was willing and able to join us."

"And do what?" Garrett pressed. "Be the evening assistant manager? Do they need an assistant manager on every
shift? Seems like bloated staffing, if you ask me."

Shelby refrained from pointing out the obvious: that no
one had asked Garrett "Cut Rate" McGrath anything. Yet
he was the one doing all the asking, and offensively, too.

She glanced from Paul's immaculate summer suit to
Garrett's inappropriate cutoffs and hideous banana yellow
T-shirt imprinted with bright oranges and a palm tree, with
Florida emblazed over the tacky scene in multicolored letters. She didn't allow herself to concentrate on his muscular build or to remember the virile strength of him when he'd
held her in his arms. She didn't dare let her eyes linger on his
hard, sensuous mouth or his deep, dark blue eyes. And most
of all, she refused to even think about those impulsive,

tempestuous kisses they'd shared in the ocean that morning.

Instead, she concentrated on his offending attire. No one wore jeans at Halford House, and as for his T-shirt . . . such an item had to have been purchased at an airport gift shop at best, or at worst, from one of those tourist-trap junk shops littering the coast. Thank goodness such places had not infected unspoiled Port Key—yet.

Shelby had a sudden horrible thought. "You're not thinking of trying to build a Family Fun Inn here on the island, are you?"

Was this his standard operating procedure? she wondered nervously. To come to a resort as an "observer" while casing the surrounding area like a burglar planning a follow-up sneak attack? She didn't know, Shelby realized. She knew nothing of how Garrett McGrath and his ever-successful Family Fun Inns broke into a new market. Her lack of knowledge suddenly seemed a dangerous oversight.

"Where did that non sequitur come from?" Garrett asked, amused. "Oh, wait, let me guess. You were giving my T-shirt the evil eye. . . . It naturally follows that your thoughts would jump from tacky T-shirt stands to Family Fun Inns."

"The presence of a Family Fun Inn would devalue Halford House, perhaps even leading to a similar crisis which befell the Blue Springs Resort," Paul Whitley said in alarm. "When the masses descend, they demand their usual prole vacation trappings—the junk food and souvenir places, the water slides and miniature golf." He shuddered, as if discussing a particularly gory mass murder.

"I seem to be experiencing a case of déjà vu," Garrett said dryly. "I had this same conversation with Shelby earlier this morning. Don't you high-end types talk about anything else? How about the weather? Or the local ball club?"

"You didn't answer my question, Garrett," Shelby pressed, anxiety gnawing at her. "Are you planning to put a Family Fun Inn here on Port Key?"

He liked the sound of his name on her lips, Garrett decided. This was the first time she'd addressed him as such and it pleased him that she was beginning to think of him on a first-name basis, though he doubted that she was aware of it herself.

His lips quirked. "No, Shelby, I promise I am not planning to put a Family Fun Inn anywhere near Port Key or Halford House."

It was a vow he could make with a clear conscience. He and Art Halford had signed the sale papers at lunch. He now owned Halford House. There was no way he was going to bring in a Family Fun Inn to compete with his own property.

"I wish I could believe you," Shelby murmured worriedly.

"I'll provide you with a sworn affidavit signed in blood, if you'd like. I, Garrett McGrath, do solemnly swear to keep Port Key free from Family Fun."

"Gentleman's word of honor?" Paul Whitley suggested, offering his hand to shake.

Garrett shook his hand. It would have been churlish not to. But Whitley still irritated him. "What's Halford House to you, Whitley? You never did get around to telling me."

"Paul is going to be my assistant, my right-hand man, so to speak, when my father retires," Shelby hastily replied.

Couldn't the man speak for himself? Garrett was tempted to ask. He didn't, though. Shelby would probably answer for him again. His respect for Whitley plummeted further.

"And when is your father planning to retire, Shelby?" Garrett asked curiously, his eyes gleaming. He knew the answer, of course. But what fiction had Halford told his daughter? This should be interesting; old Art had proven himself a creative liar.

Shelby and Paul exchanged uncomfortable glances. "We don't know the exact date of my father's retirement," she confessed reluctantly. "But it will be soon, Mother assured me. She and Dad want to move to Arizona. We have relatives out there."

"Your father's brother Hal, his wife Hillary, and their loafer parasite of a son who wanted no part of a career in

Halford House," Garrett added knowledgeably. "Your dad has mentioned them."

Arthur Halford had ranted on and on about his "idiot nephew," blaming his indolent lack of interest in the business as the reason for the sale of Halford House. Garrett stared at Shelby, who currently looked the part of the quintessential business executive in her no-nonsense gray suit, cheerless beige blouse buttoned to the neck, and sensible gray pumps. She was even wearing hose, no matter that the temperature was in the high eighties and stickily humid. Her hair was pulled back tightly into an uninviting, untouchable chignon.

Garrett compared her to the laughing, soft, sexy version of her that he'd been with on the beach. Instead of being turned off, he found that the two disparate sides of her further intrigued him.

"Cousin Hal has been something of a disappointment," Shelby admitted. "His brother Hart was the designated successor and when he died, everyone expected Hal Junior to step into his shoes. He didn't, but I'm here to do the job," she added brightly.

Garrett frowned thoughtfully. He knew Arthur Halford hadn't asked his daughter to take over Halford House, despite her hotel training and experience. In fact, Halford hadn't given Shelby a thought at all until she had announced that she was coming back. Then he'd panicked, but never wavered about selling. When he had signed the papers today, Halford had eagerly agreed to let Garrett tell Shelby about the sale whenever he deemed necessary, abdicating even that responsibility to someone else. The Halfords seemed oddly lacking in family loyalty, never mind family fun.

"And Paul is going to help me run Halford House and continue its success into the next century," Shelby announced, smiling enthusiastically at Paul.

Her smile annoyed Garrett, as did her marketing spiel.

"But right now, Paul is essentially unemployed?" Garrett just couldn't let that one pass. "He's living here, gratis?"

"Not gratis. I'm learning the ropes," Paul said rather defensively. "Shelby and I have put in full days, making plans and—"

"So you're both on the payroll, the once-and-future executive here and her liege?" surmised Garrett.

"That's none of your business," Shelby snapped.

"Oh, I think it is." Garrett grimaced wryly. "It most definitely is."

"Observing the way Halford House is run is one thing, but requesting confidential, financial information is something else entirely," Shelby informed him frostily.

Garrett sighed. "From your point of view, I suppose that's a valid point. But humor me by confirming a wild guess—that Art put you both on the payroll when you arrived here in Port Key last week. Am I right?"

"Oh, for goodness' sake, yes, you're right," Paul said, his voice rising with exasperation. "I don't know why you're so intent on knowing, but I have no problem revealing that I am being paid for my expertise."

"I guess I'm just insatiable for information about these five-star resorts," Garrett said dryly. Naturally, Halford had put Shelby and Whitley on the payroll immediately. He was selling the place and its payroll and expenses to the Mc-Graths. Let them pay!

"Now it's my turn to go out on a limb and make a wild guess," Paul exclaimed. "I think you're planning on going into the exclusive resort business yourself, McGrath."

Garrett stared at him, askance. The guy was not as stupid as he'd thought, despite the boyish grin, blond locks and eye-popping pastel suit. He looked at Shelby and found her staring at him. His silence had extended a moment too long, giving himself away.

"Paul's right! You are!" she gasped. Color was rising in her cheeks.

If she were to find out here and now that he'd bought Halford House, Garrett knew she would hate him forever. He thought of their time together on the beach this morning, verbally sparring, playing in the water, kissing passionately....

He wanted more, much more. He studied Shelby, his blue eyes assessing. She was bright, edgy and defensive. He had no doubts that she would be difficult to get close to. But he wanted to try. And he would never have that chance if things were ended between them right now, before they'd ever actually begun. He decided then and there he wouldn't let it happen.

"Shelby," he said tentatively, mentally preparing a defense.

Fortunately, the loquacious Paul Whitley, who'd gotten him into this mess, spoke up again. And neatly got him out.

"You're going to buy the Blue Springs Resort, aren't you?" Whitley said excitedly. "It all makes sense now—why you want firsthand information about running a top-of-the-line place. And your method of acquiring one was nothing short of ingenious! You put that cheap motel of yours next to the Blue Springs and its property value sunk into the pits. Now you're going to buy it for a song and attempt to ressurect it to its former glory."

Garrett chuckled. "Whitley, you're a sharp one. You're wasted as an evening assistant manager. You should be running a place like this. Or the Blue Springs," he added slyly.

And that's all it took. For the rest of the tour Paul was deferential and downright charming to Garrett, a virtual wealth of information about the high-end resort business. And filled with suggestions about how to restore an exclusive resort to its former pinnacle.

Shelby was irked. Paul's tactics were so obvious that it was embarrassing. He had decided that the opportunity to run the Blue Springs for Garrett McGrath was more lucrative and prestigious than serving as her second in command here at Halford House, and he was pulling out all stops to let Garrett know that he was up to the task.

She glanced resentfully at Garrett. This was all his doing. Unknowingly or not, he'd driven a wedge between her and Paul. Nothing was going as she'd originally planned, she acknowledged glumly. She and Paul had not grown closer since their arrival here. Their platonic, professional relationship remained the same as it had been in California, except two complications had been added—the entrancing Laney and now the alluring possibility of him running the Blue Springs Resort for Garrett McGrath.

Worse, her father had not mentioned his retirement and he had not turned over a single responsibility to her at Halford House. Her dreams of triumphantly taking over the family business, partnered by a man she admired and respected as a coequal, were beginning to seem depressingly elusive.

"You're awfully quiet," Garrett remarked to her as Paul led them through the gardens, expansively remarking on how similar horticultural wonders could be achieved at the Blue Springs.

"With Paul auditioning for you, I couldn't get a word in even if I wanted to," she retorted under her breath. "Which I do not. I have nothing to say to you, Mr. McGrath."

"What about our little episode of splendor-in-the-sea? Are you going to pretend it never happened?"

To her great consternation, Shelby blushed. "Be quiet!" she admonished. "Paul will hear you."

"And you don't want him to know about us?"

"There is no *us!*" Shelby shrieked.

Paul stopped talking and turned around. "What's going on?" he asked, looking from Shelby to Garrett.

The pair exchanged glances—hers threatening, his mocking.

"Nothing," Shelby snapped. She glared at Garrett, daring him to contradict her.

Garrett merely shrugged. "We were talking about that tropical storm in the Caribbean. Think it'll turn into a hurricane and head our way?"

"I hope not." Paul grimaced. "We never had to worry about hurricanes in California."

"Yeah, you had earthquakes to look forward to out there," said Garrett. "I'm concerned about the storm because Shelby and I are going to drive south to Key West tomorrow to the Family Fun Inn down there. Since she's been so generous with her time, taking me around Halford House and all, I thought I'd reciprocate and show her the workings of one of the inns."

Shelby stifled an outraged gasp. What kind of game was Garrett McGrath playing? Whatever it was, she was not a participant and it was time to let him know it.

"I'm afraid I'm going to have to refuse your kind invitation, Mr. McGrath," Shelby replied at once. Keeping her voice calm and courteous was a stretch, but she was pleased she achieved it. She was fairly certain that losing her temper would award him the winning round.

"That's it?" Garrett's smile was baiting. "A simple polite refusal? No 'I'm not interested in going anywhere with you, Mr. McGrath'? Not even an 'I wouldn't go near one of your vulgar motels unless I was forced at gunpoint'? I'm disappointed, Shelby. Are you losing your edge?"

Paul Whitley stared from one to the other in uneasy silence. Both Shelby and Garrett seemed oblivious to his presence as they faced each other down like two gunslingers ready to shoot it out in the Old West.

Garrett looked away first but before Shelby could relish her small victory, he made it clear that he wasn't conceding, merely regrouping. "Your parents invited me to have dinner with them and you and your sister tonight. We'll continue our discussion about our trip then. Meanwhile, I have some business to attend to." He lightly tapped Paul's shoulder. "You're a wealth of information, Whitley. I appreciate your input."

Paul beamed.

Shelby seethed. Garrett McGrath did not play by the rules! Silently, she and Paul watched Garrett turn and walk briskly from the gardens, his confident, cocky stride setting Shelby's teeth on edge.

"I am not having dinner with him tonight," she announced. "And I most certainly will not drive to Key West with him tomorrow to visit one of his abominable motels!"

Four

———

"**Y**ou can't be serious." Garrett's eyes swept over Shelby, who stood rigidly before him. Her severely tailored brown suit, her starched ecru blouse, buttoned, naturally, right up to the neck, her darkly tinted hose and no-nonsense, low-heeled brown pumps would all be considered rather drab and stodgy even in the most conservative workplace.

For an informal tour of a Family Fun Inn in Key West, a casual place in a less-than-conservative resort town, her attire seemed more of a costume. A ridiculously inappropriate one.

"I don't know what you mean," Shelby replied coolly.

"I'm talking about that getup you're wearing. What is it? A period piece from the early '70s—the humorless feminist separatist who believed that anything with style or color was selling out?" He shook his head. "You can't wear that. You'll scare away the tourists."

"If you don't like the way I'm dressed, you can always uninvite me," Shelby suggested with saccharine sweetness.

"Not a chance," Garrett assured her. "Oh, and while you're changing clothes, do your hair a favor and set it free. Right now, it's pulled back so tight, your eyes are slanting."

Shelby faced him squarely, her hazel eyes defiant. "I'm not changing. I consider this trip strictly business and I have dressed accordingly."

Garrett shrugged. "Okay, have it your way, but you're going to be awfully uncomfortable in this heat. Don't say I didn't warn you."

"I won't say anything at all to you," she vowed. Her gaze flicked over him, critically taking in his oversize navy-and-white-striped cotton shirt, sockless boat shoes and faded blue jeans. Her lips curled scornfully. Obviously they were his business-hours jeans as they were not cut off above the knees.

She glanced at her watch and heaved an impatient sigh. "I suggest we get started. With all the traffic, it'll take close to four hours to reach Key West. The sooner we leave, the sooner this ridiculous trip will be over."

"I can already tell you're going to be good company," Garrett said dryly as he handed the valet parking attendant the ticket stub to claim his car. "The miles and the hours are going to fly by."

"I will do my best not to annoy you, and I hope you will return the courtesy," Shelby said tightly. "If that means spending the entire day without exchanging another word, so be it."

"Sorry, honey." Garrett grinned wickedly. "I'm looking forward to annoying you. Why else would I have invited you along?"

A parking attendant arrived at the entrance with a bright red two-door car, one of the smallest models Shelby had ever seen. "It's not much bigger than a toy," she exclaimed, astonished. "I think the dessert cart in our dining room is bigger than this."

"It was the smallest car the rental agency had," explained Garrett. "Whenever I rent a car, I always try to find

one I've never driven before. For variety, I use different
rental agencies and ask all of them for their oldest car or the
newest one or the smallest or largest, whatever category I
can come up with. I've had some interesting rides that way.
One time I ended up with an old hearse. Drove it all through
Kansas and Missouri.''

"Good thing you're not driving a hearse today," the attendant said, casting a meaningful glance at Shelby.

Garrett laughed heartily at that. Shelby managed to pro-
duce a synthetic smile. The two of them climbed into the
bucket seats. "I always rent a fuel-efficient compact," she
told him. "But nothing *this* compact."

"I thought you'd go for something appropriately high-
endish, in keeping with the exalted Halford House image.
Certain specialized agencies do rent expensive luxury cars,
you know."

"No, I didn't know, not that I would rent one. I am a
businesswoman, not an overindulged snob," she said
tightly. It bothered her that he saw her that way; even more
irritating was that she was bothered by it at all.

Garrett slipped the parking attendant a twenty-dollar bill
for his assistance, and the young man effusively thanked
him, beaming from ear to ear.

"You overtip," Shelby pointed out, as Garrett slowly
steered the little car along the long paved road leading out
of the Halford House grounds and back to the outside
world. "I saw you doing it last night after dinner, too,
overtipping the waitress and the busboy and the wine stew-
ard. My father had already adequately compensated them.
There was no need for you to—"

"Your father's idea of adequate compensation doesn't
jibe with mine," Garrett cut in. "In fact, there isn't much
Art Halford says or does that I agree with. For example, if
I had a daughter who so obviously did not want to go away
with a certain colleague, I would never insist that she do so.
And old Art did more than insist that you come with me.
Coercion is the term that comes to mind."

Shelby reached into her leather handbag and pulled out a tissue to wipe her forehead. Her skin was already beginning to perspire under her bangs. It was an unseasonably hot day. Although just eight o'clock in the morning, the temperature was already nearing eighty, the humidity in the unbearable range. The car had air-conditioning, but she still had to contend with the sun beating down through the windows, directly on her. Shelby discreetly opened the top two buttons of her blouse. She felt as if the starched, slender mandarin-style neck was choking her.

She cast a sidelong glance at Garrett. Due to the sun's particular angle, the driver's side of the car was spared the heat of the direct rays. His loose, short-sleeved shirt bared his muscular forearms. Unlike hers, his dark hair was not damp from sweat. Not a drop of perspiration beaded on his forehead, either. Resentment flared through her.

"Since you know I didn't want to come with you and you don't approve of my father coercing me, why did you insist that I make this stupid trip with you?" she demanded crossly. "Just to be perverse?"

"Got it on the first try!" Garrett enthused. "You're a sharp one, Shelby."

"You told Paul he was a sharp one, too," Shelby reminded him acidly. "Maybe I should start campaigning for an executive position at the Blue Springs Resort?"

"You noticed he was doing that, hmm?"

"Of course."

Garrett smiled. "You've worked with Whitley. Do you think he's capable of running a place like Halford House, or, uh, the Blue Springs? Be honest now."

"Paul is quite capable," she said stiffly. "I wouldn't have asked him to join us at Halford House if I didn't consider him to be competent and an asset to the place."

"I wondered if there was another reason why you asked him. A more personal reason." Garrett braked the car to a stop at a traffic light and looked over at her.

He caught her staring at him. For a moment their eyes met and held, then Shelby quickly looked away, her cheeks warm. She'd been stealing glances at Garrett McGrath, staring surreptitiously at him entirely too often, she admonished herself. She had done so too many times during dinner last night with Laney and her parents and him. She couldn't seem to control her straying eyes. But to have him catch her at it.... It was *mortifying!*

"Paul and I are friends and we work well together," she said, fumbling with the windshield visor in a vain attempt to shade herself from the infernal sun.

"Nothing romantic between you?" Garrett was pleased to hear her confirm what he had already guessed. But the fact remained that Shelby had invited Whitley to Florida. Garrett did not care for the implications of that.

"Are you harboring some kind of hope that something may develop between you and Whitley?" he pressed. Because if she was, he was going to crush those hopes here and now, he decided with a fierceness that surprised him.

"That is none of your business!" Shelby flared.

"If you are, you're going to be sadly disappointed. I could tell last night that your sister has designs on Whitley, and he appears to be goggle-eyed over her." Garrett slanted her a quick, assessing glance.

"Oh, please spare me your false concern. As if you care whether I'm sad or disappointed or... or enraged! Furthermore, it isn't unusual for a man to be goggle-eyed over Laney. Most men are. She's very beautiful and very charming, as you well know from dinner last night."

"Beautiful, yes." Garrett shrugged. "But being charming includes warmth and spontaneity, and I didn't find that in your sister. She did a passable imitation, but her so-called charm struck me as calculating, a performance she turns on and off at will."

His was so close to her own interpretation of Laney that Shelby was unnerved. She felt disloyal and ashamed of herself for daring to doubt the Halford family creed. "Everybody is crazy about Laney," she recited.

"I'm not," Garrett said bluntly. "She's not only phony, she's boring. It was a struggle to feign an interest in whatever it was she kept jabbering about."

"She talked about her beauty pageant days," Shelby reminded him. "And, of course, about her dogs and how much she loves animals and they love her."

"Oh, yeah." Garrett groaned in reminiscence. "It's all coming back to me now, despite my best efforts to block it out. She claimed a dolphin swam up to her in the ocean and took her for a ride on its back. She happened to be wearing her tiara from the Miss Whatever pageant at the time." He rolled his eyes. "I think she's overdosed on reruns of 'Flipper.'"

"You don't believe Laney's story?"

"Oh, come on, Shelby! Riding an untamed dolphin with a tiara on her head? If you believe that, I'll tell you about the time I was abducted by aliens and we cruised the galaxy in their spaceship. Or maybe a tale about my lunch in the Amazon jungle with a lost tribe of headhunters."

"You do lead an interesting life," Shelby said coolly. She managed to suppress the giggle that welled within her. It would be unsisterly to laugh at his derision of Laney. "Everybody thinks Laney's dolphin story is fanciful and charming," she said.

"Who is this 'everybody' you keep quoting, Shelby? Your parents? Paul Whitley? I think the reaction of most sane people when they hear Laney's own personal *Little Mermaid* story is more like 'give me a break.'"

"The light is green," Shelby replied pointedly. "You're holding up traffic."

The car behind them impatiently sounded its horn and Garrett turned his eyes back to the road.

Shelby's attention drifted to last night's dinner party with Garrett and her family. Beautiful Laney had been exuding her special brand of charm as she attempted to captivate Garrett McGrath. Garrett, however, had not been captivated. He'd treated her sister with the same friendly politeness he displayed to their mother, but directed his interest and attention to Shelby and her father, peppering the conversation with questions about Halford House and other high-end resorts, listening to their replies, seemingly filing information away in his mind for future reference.

Despite Laney's attempts to direct it otherwise, the conversation had revolved on the hotel business and rarely wavered from that course. Laney had finally cajoled Paul into taking her dancing at the resort's nightclub. Shelby had cringed when her parents jovially insisted that she and Garrett go dancing, too.

But before she'd had a chance to refuse in no uncertain terms, Garrett did it first, claiming he wanted an early night because he and Shelby were leaving in the morning for this trip to Key West.

There had been no getting out of it for her. As Garrett had said, her father had coerced her, making it clear that she was shirking her responsibilities to Halford House if she didn't accompany Mr. McGrath. And everybody knew what happened to employees whom Art Halford considered derelict in the line of duty. Shelby wasn't one to kid herself; she might be Arthur Halford's daughter, but he would deal no differently with her than any other employee who'd incurred his wrath.

And since she had been forced along on this so-called business trip, she intended to treat it as exactly that, making it obvious by her attire and her attitude that her presence meant strictly business. If Garrett McGrath thought he could lure her into another splendor-in-the-sea interlude...

Shelby felt her face grow pink as a renegade memory of herself in Garrett's arms flashed to mind. She immediately halted the direction her thoughts had taken and steered them along another, less disturbing track.

The sun continued to glare unrelentingly through the tinted windows, which were a paltry defense against the scorching rays. Reluctantly, but unable to bear it anymore, Shelby removed her suit jacket and laid it across the miniscule back seat.

"Hot enough for you?" Garrett grinned.

Her lips tightened. "I was waiting for your 'I told you so.' You didn't disappoint."

"I hope I never disappoint you, Shelby," he said, the usual note of teasing mockery absent from his voice. He directed the air-conditioning vents toward her and increased the flow of cold air to maximum capacity. "Better?" he asked.

Shelby nodded, caught off guard by his helpfulness. The man was unpredictable, an enigma. A fascinating and perceptive one. She tried to keep from glancing at him, and when she did, she tried to keep those covert glances from lingering. It was getting harder and harder to do both.

They drove along the Overseas Highway, which connected the mainland with the string of islands known as the Florida Keys. As usual, the traffic was heavy with tractor-trailers, cars towing boats, RVs, plus innumerable cars filled with tourists. Shelby had made the drive many times before, but this was Garrett's first trip on the highway that boasted forty-two bridges as it crossed the Keys and skimmed across the sea, the Atlantic Ocean on one side of it, the Gulf of Mexico on the other.

"As you might expect, I'm a big fan of billboards and fast-food stands and motels and strip malls," Garrett remarked after driving past all of them, "but I'd love to get off the highway and see something of the Keys. Hey, look at that sign for the International Fishing Museum. It says they'll help find a charter boat for deep-sea or back-country fishing. Let's do it!"

"This is a business trip," Shelby reminded him. "I'm certainly not dressed for a fishing expedition." She smoothed her skirt with her palms and gingerly eased her feet out of her pumps, which were beginning to pinch. "I've been to the museum, though. They have a large collection of antique fishing tackles that I found rather interesting."

"I'm more interested in fishing than looking at tackles, antique or not."

"I'd rather look at the tackles than charter a boat for the express purpose of luring innocent fish to their deaths."

Garrett groaned. "You're not one of those fanatics who won't eat something with a face, are you? Come to think of it, all you ate last night for dinner was a bowl of clam chowder, spinach salad and bread."

"None of which has a face," she observed. He looked so appalled that this time Shelby couldn't suppress the laughter bubbling up inside her. "No, I'm not overly zealous about what I won't eat, but I don't care to see my food in the transitional stages. You know, between life and death."

"You prefer it packaged and unrecognizable."

"Precisely."

"I guess this means you won't be joining me on my annual fall hunting trip?"

"How true."

"Say, what do you do for fun, anyway? We've already established that you don't hunt or fish or swim in the ocean in your clothes. Your runs on the beach are part of your serious exercise regime and not done for pleasure. So what about your leisure time? Do you ever just kick back and relax?"

Shelby shifted uneasily. "I'm not very good at relaxing," she admitted reluctantly. "Oh, I enjoy reading and the occasional television show—"

"Only public television, of course. You probably don't approve of network or cable fare."

"You make me sound like a stuffy old maid." Shelby grimaced. "Like that awful old crone pictured in the card game! Well, I suppose my life does seem awfully boring to someone like you." Her face was burning—and not from the sun's glare.

"I'm not exactly a fast-living, high-roller, party animal, either," Garrett confessed. "Most of my time is devoted to business. Building the company, keeping it growing and successful hasn't left a whole lot of time for a wild social life. And in my spare time, I prefer being outdoors to reading or television. Even public television." His blue eyes gleamed.

She felt ridiculously relieved that he wasn't a fixture on the party circuit. "I really prefer working to anything else," she confided. "At the Casa del Marina, I was on duty more than I was off and I liked it that way."

"You must be going crazy at Halford House," Garrett remarked. "From what I've gathered, your father hasn't given you much to do since your return."

His perception rankled but she couldn't deny it. "No, my father hasn't found a place for me yet." It was a painful admission for her to make. "But I expect that to change," she added, lifting her chin, proudly defiant.

"And if it doesn't? Suppose your father decides to sell Halford House when he retires? What will you do then?"

"I don't believe in worrying about something that will never happen," Shelby said confidently. "Halford House has been in the family for three generations and it'll stay in the family for many more."

Garrett thought of Arthur Halford's willingness to sell Halford House, his eagerness to finalize the deal. He'd disposed of the Halford heritage without a thought, until his elder daughter's inconvenient arrival back on the scene. Even then, Halford hadn't reconsidered the sale, not for a moment. His only concern was to keep Shelby in the dark until a more convenient time presented itself for breaking the news. And then the old man had even abdicated on that, passing the unpleasant task on to the new owner himself.

It wasn't going to be easy, Garrett admitted with an inward groan. The more time he spent with Shelby, the more he realized how very difficult it would be to tell her that her father had sold out the family business without giving a thought to her own plans and dreams of running the place. And when she learned that Garrett McGrath of Family Fun Inns had bought the place...

His fingers tightened on the wheel. His interest in Shelby had begun as a lark, a bit of spontaneous curiosity, but it was rapidly developing into something else entirely. Something complicated and involved. And while he thrived on complicated and involved challenges in business, he carefully avoided such traps in his personal life.

Until now. He should have known he was in trouble the moment Shelby had burst into Art Halford's office, Garrett acknowledged. He'd felt something deep inside him respond to her on sight. And he finally admitted to himself that if he hadn't felt that almost primal attraction to her, he would've refused to go along with Halford's plan to deceive his daughter. He would have played it the usual Garrett McGrath way—blunt, open and forceful—and told her the truth then and there.

Garrett rarely felt the need to confide in others but he made it a point to be honest with himself. He wanted Shelby Halford. He wanted her soft and warm and laughing as she'd been in the ocean yesterday. He wanted her hungry and responsive, clinging to him in passion. He even wanted her, taut and edgy, in her staid business suit, prim hairdo and orthopedic panty hose. She intrigued him. She was intelligent and driven, witty and sensual when she wanted to be. When he inspired her to be.

In the seat beside him, Shelby was fighting a losing battle to keep her eyes trained to the window and the passing sights outside. Her gaze kept straying to Garrett, sliding over the dark thickness of his hair, his strong implacable profile. And then lower. To his hard-muscled arms and his big hands capably gripping the steering wheel. She swallowed, her mouth suddenly quite dry.

"You're awfully quiet all of a sudden," Shelby said nervously.

"So are you."

She actually blushed. Had he noticed that she'd been staring at him again? On the other hand, if he'd caught her looking at him, that meant he had been looking at her, too. She recognized the embers of sexual excitement flaring within her for exactly what they were.

And tried hard to tamp them with a stern, no-nonsense lecture to herself about the folly of developing a schoolgirl crush on Garrett McGrath. She was no longer a schoolgirl and Garrett was a man with his own agenda. He was a man who always seemed to get what he wanted—such as all those Family Fun Inns in places where others had worked to keep them out. Their efforts had been futile and Garrett Mc-Grath had always prevailed.

Shelby remembered their brief ocean idyll yesterday. Somehow she'd ended up frolicking fully dressed in the water with him—she who'd *never* frolicked anywhere in her entire life! And then he had grabbed her and kissed her and she had responded with every fiber of her being.

Heat shimmered through her. Yes, Garrett McGrath got whatever he wanted. He was a dangerous man and she would do well to remember it. And to keep both her eyes and her thoughts away from him.

They drove across the Seven Mile Bridge leading to the Lower Keys and, finally, to the southernmost island of Key West. Garrett tossed Shelby a city map and she directed him to the Family Fun Inn, which he'd circled in ink.

"It's near Dog Beach," she remarked. "That's the only beach in Key West where dogs are allowed. Did you choose the location for that reason? Do most of your patrons travel with their pets?"

"A number of our inns have kennel facilities. Hmm, do you think Halford House should provide canine and feline accommodations? The rich and famous are as devoted to their pets as anybody else."

"Why don't you try it out at the Blue Springs?" Shelby suggested sweetly. "Install kennels there. We at Halford House will be eagerly awaiting the test results."

Garrett frowned. Shelby believed he was buying the Blue Springs Resort. He'd momentarily forgotten that piece of fiction. He debated telling her here and now that he was not buying the Blue Springs at all, but rather, that the Mc-Graths' venture into the high-end market of the hotel business comprised the purchase of Halford House.

He pulled the car into a parking space in front of Key West's Family Fun Inn and turned to Shelby. She'd put her jacket and shoes back on and was dabbing powder on her nose. She looked tense and uptight, uncomfortable and hot. Definitely unreachable. It stood to reason that while in such a mood she would not be very receptive to the news about the sale of Halford House. In fact, she might be quite unreasonable about it—and even less understanding about the deception surrounding it.

Garrett made up his mind. He wouldn't tell her. Not yet. She would have to find out eventually, of course, but not until the time was right. And he would know when and where that would be. One thing was certain. It wasn't now.

"Well, this is it," he announced as they climbed out of the car and stood in front of the motel. "Welcome to the Family Fun Inn."

Shelby stared at the white wood and concrete block structure with its row of rooms on the upper and lower levels. The door to each room was painted a different color and there didn't seem to be a single shade they'd missed. Shelby blinked at the brilliant purples and pinks and oranges and limes. The primary colors were well represented, too, with bright yellows, blues and reds.

For a few minutes she was silent, rather awed by the vivid sight. As much as she'd heard about Family Fun Inns, she had never actually seen one with her own eyes.

She tried to imagine the reaction of the owners of the understated, elegant Blue Springs Resort when the painters had finished with the new, unwanted Family Fun Inn that had sprung up next door to it. It was a sure bet they hadn't been pleased.

Garrett watched her expectantly. He seemed to be waiting for her to make some comment. "It looks like a giant crayon box," she said at last.

"That's exactly the effect we wanted." He nodded his approval. "Kids love colors and we've found from our market research that they have very particular ideas concerning the different colored doors. Some children are attached to one certain color, and at every Family Fun Inn they want a room with that same favorite colored door. Other kids like to collect different colors. They want to stay behind a different colored door every time they come. So we ask our guests for their door color preference when they make reservations or check in.''

"It sounds scarily like your penchant for selecting rental cars. Collecting rides in different rental cars is bizarre enough, but collecting stays behind different colored doors is even stranger. Who cares if the room you're staying in has a turquoise door or an orchid door or a chartreuse door?'' She did not add that all were equally garish, but the thought crossed her mind.

"Kids care. And on a family trip, their parents are willing to indulge them. It's a gimmick that has ensured us so much repeat business that other chains have stopped laughing, checked their occupancy rates and ours, and are trying to come up with something similar.''

Shelby gazed at the dazzling array of colors lined up before her. "We can only hope they never will,'' she murmured under her breath.

Garrett identified himself to Tony Fontana, the motel manager, who seemed genuinely thrilled to meet the big boss at last.

"Your sister Fiona and her husband and their children were down last year, and I've also met Grace and Jeff, and, of course, Eilish,'' the manager exclaimed effusively. "Will you be staying here at the motel tonight, Mr. McGrath?''

Fontana slanted a discreet glance at Shelby, though not so discreet that she didn't see it and interpret it. He thought she was the big boss's bimbo!

Five

    —

"No, we will not be spending the night," Shelby replied at once. "This is a business trip," she felt compelled to add. How many times had she said that today? It had practically become her rallying cry. She glared at Tony Fontana. Weren't her professional demeanor and her attire unmistakable clues that she was Garrett's colleague and not his bedmate du jour? It wasn't as if she'd shown up in a halter top and spandex miniskirt, dripping with costume jewelry and a wad of pink bubble gum in her mouth.

"How many vacancies do you have tonight, Tony?" Garrett asked smoothly, breeching the sudden awkward silence that had fallen.

"We have just one room available tonight, sir, but—"

"You're at full occupancy except for one room?" Shelby interjected incredulously. Astonishment overrode her annoyance as she considered the sizable vacancy at Halford House. Was Tony Fontana padding the occupancy rate to impress the boss? It was the off-season, after all.

"We're always at full occupancy, ma'am," Tony Fontana said politely. "At twenty-nine dollars a night, we get a lot of families with very young children not yet in school. They like the off-season because they can avoid the crowds that go with school vacations. We're popular with retirees, as well, and they tend to travel during both the on and off seasons."

"We're starting to get some business travelers, too," Garrett added. "They're just beginning to discover us."

"Can you imagine landing even a small portion of that market?" Tony mused, his expression wistful.

"Yes, I can imagine it," Garrett replied confidently. "It's going to happen within the next couple years and we'll profit immensely, but we won't lose our commitment to family vacationers."

Shelby listened absently to the exchange, still stupefied by Fontana's incredible revelation. "Your rooms are twenty-nine dollars a night." She said it aloud. That price didn't even cover the cost of lunch for two at Halford House.

"All Family Fun Inns are twenty-nine dollars a night, plus tax," Garrett explained. "Except during our discount promotions. Then they're less."

"But Key West is an expensive area, the costs are higher here for everything than on the mainland. How do you make a profit? How do you stay in business?" demanded Shelby.

"We have constant, continual occupancy and we keep our overhead costs to the bare minimum," Fontana said proudly. "Having this one room available tonight is a fluke, due to an unexpected cancellation. Tomorrow, we'll be totally booked, as usual."

"You're doing a terrific job here, Tony," Garrett assured him. "My sisters couldn't stop singing your praises after their visits here. I wanted to get down and see for myself."

Shelby followed the two men into the manager's office and took a chair farthest from the window, out of range of the sun's glare. She listened as they discussed the company's latest advertising campaign and a new cooperative arrangement between Family Fun Inns and eight different airlines, in which frequent-flier miles were awarded to those guests who stayed in any Family Fun Inn. They talked about a pizza chain that delivered free of charge to the motel rooms and the possibility of working out a similar arrangement with a local burger franchise.

She got a glimpse of Garrett's management style. He was warm and empowering, objective yet emphatic. And smart, very smart. Garrett McGrath was the man who had built Family Fun Inns into the successful empire it was today. He was the chief executive who kept it running at a profit when so many hotels and motels were floundering for their niche in the recessionary market. He might not dress the part, but he was as shrewd a businessman as any blue blood who vacationed at Halford House.

"What color is the door of the only available room?" Garrett asked suddenly.

The question struck Shelby as inane and she almost laughed out loud. She was glad she hadn't when Tony Fontana treated the inquiry with utmost gravity.

"Green." The manager seemed truly grieved. "Green is always the least requested color and the last to be rented."

Garrett nodded. "I know. It's the same throughout the chain. Why is the green the least popular? Kind of strange, hmm?" He slanted a glance at Shelby. "Even more strange is that green happens to be the theme color at Halford House. Could there possibly be some paradoxical connection? Why is Halford green a hit and Family Fun green a miss?"

"A mystery indeed!" Fontana took the question seriously. "Do you think we should do a study?"

"What's strangest of all is that grown men are pondering the appeal of green doors," Shelby said succinctly. "Who cares?"

Fontana looked shocked. Garrett merely smiled. "She would drive our marketing team nuts, eh, Tony? Come on, let's show her what one of our rooms looks like."

Shelby traipsed after them, through the least-popular, least-requested green door into a medium-size bedroom. It was furnished with sturdy, utilitarian furniture and decorated with a plain functional bedspread and matching curtains and rugs. There was an adjacent bathroom, equipped with soap and towels, a plastic ice bucket and drinking glasses. Nothing else. No shampoo or lotion, no shower caps or sewing kit or razors, none of the countless toiletry and grooming items routinely stocked in every Halford House bathroom.

"We save costs by cutting out everything but the bare essentials," Garrett remarked, as if reading her mind.

"We do have color TV with cable hookup," Tony Fontana said loyally.

"Of course." Shelby nodded. "What family could have fun without TV?"

Tony glanced uncertainly at Garrett, awaiting his reaction. When Garrett chuckled, so did he.

"She catches on quick, doesn't she, Tony? Think there's a place for her in the organization?"

Fontana looked so bemused that Shelby took pity on him. "Don't answer that, Tony," she advised. He nodded gratefully.

According to Garrett, the pride of every Family Fun Inn was its playground, an elaborate, unique park on the grounds of the motel. Along with the usual swings and jungle gyms was original equipment guaranteed to delight the young motel guests, such as a bright green-and-yellow crocodile whose pink tongue was a slide, a playhouse shaped like a castle, a merry-go-ground designed like a spaceship.

"My sister Fiona's husband, Ray, designs and builds playgrounds," Garrett explained. "Family Fun Inns is his number one client but he has other markets, too—schools and community centers and the like. His company is very successful. Fiona and Ray have two kids, three-year-old twin boys."

"You can see for yourself how much the children love this playground," Tony Fontana said with proprietary pride.

"We don't have swimming pools at Family Fun Inns, which cuts maintenance and liability costs, but our playgrounds are first-rate."

The playground was filled with small children, squealing and laughing under their parents' watchful eyes. "They look so happy," Shelby murmured wistfully, gazing at the cheerful scene.

Had she ever been as carefree and merry as those bright-eyed children? She doubted it. Her memories of herself as a child were of a serious, driven little girl, compulsive in her need to achieve, distraught and furious with any perceived failure.

"At Family Fun Inns, our goal is making families happy," Tony Fontana announced proudly.

"Our corporate motto," Garrett explained. "Well said, Tony."

Shelby had no snide comeback. These people were having fun and she didn't begrudge them a moment of it.

After bidding goodbye to a pleased Tony, Garrett suggested having lunch before heading back to Port Key. Shelby realized at that moment she was starving. She hadn't eaten since breakfast and not much then. She'd been too angry about this enforced trip. But she wasn't angry any longer, she realized.

"I guess this trip hasn't been as heinous as I thought it would be," she said, as Garrett escorted her into a crowded seafood bar on the Mallory Dock.

"Such effusive praise," Garrett said dryly. "Careful, it'll go to my head. And as Grandmother McGrath is fond of saying, 'When the head swells, the brain stops working.' She used to repeat it like a litany to me."

"She considered it her duty to keep you humble? That must have been a full-time job for the poor old woman."

Garrett laughed. "It used to be. Being the oldest son, I was adored by my parents and I saw no reason to doubt their high opinion of me. Good thing I had Gran to keep me grounded in reality or I might've grown up to be totally insufferable." His tone and his laughing blue eyes were baiting her.

Shelby couldn't resist the lure. "Instead, you grew up to be merely *somewhat* insufferable. A modest victory for the ego-busting Grandmother McGrath."

"Gran has since joined my fan club. When the inns became successful and her stock in the company made her a rich woman, she decided that perhaps I wasn't such an irredeemable hellion, after all. She's currently turned her wrath on my kid brother Brendan. Lucky for him, he goes to school in New Mexico, far away from Buffalo and Gran's laser tongue."

"He's the latest McGrath irredeemable hellion?" Shelby surmised, amused.

"I wouldn't call him that. He's a college student, a real outgoing kid who—"

"Translation—Brendan is majoring in partying," Shelby said dryly. "Anytime I heard the family describe Laney and Hal Junior as 'real outgoing kids,' I knew they'd flunked another course."

Garrett gave his head a rueful shake. "Let's just say that Brendan would rather party and play golf than study. But there is a silver lining in the cloud of his grade-point average. Brendan is an excellent golfer and his goal is to be a golf pro at a club or resort. I can see him fitting in very nicely at—"

Garrett abruptly broke off and reached for his menu. He'd almost blown it again. Complicated schemes of deceit might be Arthur Halford's forte, but they were not his own.

"Blue Springs has a wonderful golf course," Shelby said knowingly. "Not quite as good as the one at Halford House but, of course, I'm prejudiced. Is that why you bought the Blue Springs Resort? So your little brother will—"

"I keep my role as head of the company separate from my role of big brother," Garrett said brusquely. "I would never make a business decision based on personal reasons. When I acquire property, it's for sound business reasons based on research and a guaranteed profit."

Shelby eyed him curiously. "I think I hit a nerve."

He studied his menu intently, as if he were going to be quizzed on the contents.

"Your usual jokes and smirks seem to be missing when it comes to discussing your recent acquisition of the Blue Springs Resort. But there's no need to be defensive about your foray into the high-end market, Garrett. I think it's sweet that you're so concerned about your little brother's future you would actually buy the Blue—"

"I am not sweet," Garrett said, frowning forbiddingly at her. "And I'm sick of talking about the Blue Springs Resort. I refuse to discuss it anymore."

"So if I keep talking about the Blue Springs, you won't talk to me? If I bring up their menu, which incidentally, has slipped drastically in the past couple years, you won't have any response? You'll sit there in stony silence?"

"I would never be so boorish as to sit in stony silence when there is a beautiful woman seated across the table from me." He flashed a heart-stopping smile. "I'll simply redirect the conversation."

Shelby felt the impact of his warm blue-eyed gaze deep inside her where tiny hot sparks erupted into a fiery stab of sensual awareness. She was instantly back on her guard. The man was indeed dangerous when his smile evoked such a reaction from her. And he'd called her a beautiful woman. Though she knew she wasn't and was aware that such talk was standard smooth-operator jargon, it was still an effective line. Embarrassingly effective. Laney might take such a remark for granted but it brought a flush of guilty pleasure to Shelby's cheeks.

"What are you having for lunch?" Garrett asked casually, glancing back at the menu.

She wouldn't allow him to manipulate her, Shelby decided. And he was *not* going to redirect the conversation. "The Blue Springs had a marvelous riding stable," she replied instead. "I was always envious of it, but my father hates horses and refused to even consider having stables at

Halford House. What are your plans for the Blue Springs stables when you take over the place?''

"Looks like conch is the main feature on the menu," Garrett remarked, as if she hadn't spoken at all. "Conch chowder, conch salad, conch fritters. What's this—conch ravioli? I think I'll try all of it."

"When will the sale of the Blue Springs be announced?" Shelby continued her own course of this parallel conversation. "Obviously it's a secret but nothing stays secret in the industry for long."

"Which only reinforces the crux of my dilemma," Garrett said wryly. "This is a subject that I can't discuss with you in good faith at this particular time, Shelby."

She didn't know the half of it! He searched for a way to break the news about the sale of Halford House that wouldn't break her heart and send her storming out of his life forever. But he couldn't come up with one. His lips tightened into a frown.

"Oh, all right, I'll stop asking you for information about the Blue Springs," Shelby conceded with a sigh. "After all, it is your business, not mine."

"Thank you," Garrett said with genuine relief. The more she quizzed him about the Blue Springs Resort, the sooner she would draw the logical conclusion that he didn't know a thing about the place. And that would certainly alert her suspicions. What kind of businessman bought a property he had zero knowledge of?

"However, I would like to remind you that you have no compunction about hounding me for facts about Halford House," Shelby stated succinctly.

"When I seek information, it's hounding, but when you do it, it's merely *asking?*" Garrett's mouth curved wryly.

Shelby arched her dark eyebrows. "Since this is your first visit to Key West, by all means indulge in conch. It's the island specialty. I myself am going to have the turtle chowder and blacktip shark."

"Point taken. We'll move on to a totally neutral topic. The weather. Are those storm clouds gathering off to the south?"

Shelby glanced out the window, saw the dark clouds in the distance and shrugged. "Afternoon storms often blow in quickly and are over just as fast in the Keys."

"I hope it does rain, just to get a break from this heat and humidity." Garrett fanned himself with the menu. "It's hard to cool down, even inside."

Shelby was beyond fanning. She removed her suit jacket, draping it across an empty chair, unfastened another button on her blouse, then undid the cuffs and rolled the sleeves to her elbows.

Garrett didn't even say "I told you so."

They had such a good time at lunch—laughing and talking easily together, relaxing and enjoying the delicious food—that Shelby didn't hesitate when Garrett suggested a tour of the town. She was in no real hurry to get back to Halford House because there was nothing there that required her presence this afternoon. She did not take her reasoning one step further—that she was in no hurry at all to end this afternoon with Garrett.

"But before we go anywhere..." Garrett took her arm and guided her into a large souvenir shop that sold everything from T-shirts, pinwheels, sand buckets and shells to horrid, mummified baby alligators dressed in doll-size clothes.

Shelby stared at the reptiles in fascinated disgust. "You aren't going to buy one of those?" she asked when Garrett lifted one up to check the price.

"It's tempting, but this time I'll pass. I'm here for something else." He started toward the back of the shop. "You look around, I'll be with you in a few minutes."

Shelby wandered through the aisles, awed by the sheer tackiness of some of the merchandise that shared space with practical items like sunscreens, sunglasses and postcards. There was a rack of paperback books, and she was study-

ing the titles when Garrett rejoined her, carrying a paper
bag.

They walked outside. "Here." He handed her the bag.
"For you."

Her eyes widened. If he'd actually bought her a dead,
dressed baby alligator or a plastic snow globe as a memento
of the day, she was going to have to politely thank him. After all, one person's junk was another one's treasure, or
something to that effect. She peeked tentatively inside the
bag.

"It's...clothes?" Shelby pulled out pink, green and white
plaid boxer-style shorts and a pink T-shirt. There was also
a pair of pink rubber flip-flops.

"You can change in the restroom of the restaurant across
the street." Garrett's suggestion sounded more like an order.

"I can't let you buy me clothes," Shelby protested.

"Not even cheap ones from a tacky souvenir shop?"

"Garrett, if I wanted these I could've bought them for
myself."

"True. But you didn't know you wanted them. You didn't
even know that you needed them. And you do, Shelby.
You'll melt in the heat in that getup—uh, outfit—you're
wearing now."

He had a point. The temperature had soared into the
midnineties and Shelby was perspiring merely by standing
still outside the shop. She would certainly be cooler if she
were to shed these layers of clothes. And the shorts and T-
shirt he'd selected weren't hideous, although the pink flip-
flops were another matter entirely. But at this point they
would be more comfortable than the too-tight heels on her
swollen feet and the sweltering panty hose. "All right, but
I insist on paying you back for them."

"If you insist, I'll accept," Garrett said graciously, his
blue eyes twinkling.

She went back into the store and bought a multicolored
cloth ponytail holder. Her scalp was beginning to ache from
the strain of her tightly bound chignon and a loose ponytail
would be a relief from both the pressure and the heat.

They stowed her business clothes in the cramped back seat of the little car and headed for the Hemingway House, now a museum dedicated to the novelist's life and work.

"You look great," Garrett said, eyeing her long bare legs with open appreciation as they walked toward the entrance.

"These are cut too short." Shelby tugged at the hem of the plaid boxers but it did little good. She felt self-conscious and overexposed. She never wore very short shorts like these, not even for running on the beach.

"I repeat, you look great." This time he gave a comical, lascivious leer.

She couldn't help laughing; his expression was exaggerated and ridiculous. Garrett reached for her hand and tucked it into his own.

She shouldn't have laughed, Shelby scolded herself. Her laughter had encouraged him and this man certainly did not need encouragement. He was already fully aware of his own charm and appeal.

And she was achingly aware of the strength of his big hand enfolding hers.

Garrett felt her small tremor at his touch and a surge of pure male possessiveness flashed through him. Her fingers were slim and graceful, her hand small and feminine. He wanted her. And she was very sensually aware of him, too, he was certain of that. How long would it take for him to make her want him?

He thought of their passionate kisses in the ocean yesterday. Not long, he promised himself. Not long at all. Ruefully aware of his semiaroused state, he forced his thoughts away from his body—and hers—and back to their surroundings, the two-story Spanish Colonial-style house where Ernest Hemingway had lived and wrote. And raised cats.

"Good God, there must be a hundred cats around here!" Garrett was amazed by the sheer numbers of feline inhabitants.

"Forty-two," amended Shelby knowledgeably. "For the forty-two bridges in the Keys. They're all descendants of

Hemingway's own fifty cats. Kittens are available for adoption but there's a fee and a waiting list."

One of the cats strolled over to them and rubbed against Shelby's ankles, seeking attention. When she stooped to pat its big striped head, it began to purr.

"He picked you out of the crowd," Garrett remarked. "Positive proof of your sheer animal magnetism. I guess both you and Laney possess it. She attracts dolphins and you attract cats."

"And you attract..." Shelby began playfully. She was going to say T-shirt shops and video arcades, miniature golf courses and motels for the masses.

"You?" Garrett interrupted. "I hope." His voice was teasing but his blue eyes were intent. She was still crouched down, petting the cat, and he slipped his hands under her arms and half lifted her to her feet.

A hushed stillness seemed to fall, encapsulating them both. For a long moment they stood there together, their bodies close but not touching, his hands gripping her, their gazes locked.

Shelby's heart was pounding and her thoughts careered through her brain like pieces of loose shrapnel. He was going to kiss her, right here and now, in broad daylight, in front of Ernest Hemingway's house with a plethora of tourists and cats milling around.

"Garrett, no," she heard herself say. Her voice was husky but decisive. The bonds of restraint she had placed on herself through the years were too strong and too tight for her to break. A kiss on a deserted beach had been risqué enough; a kiss in the middle of a crowded tourist attraction was absolutely unacceptable.

Garrett dropped his hands but not before sliding them along the length of her torso, pausing to caress the curves of her hips. Then he straightened and shoved his hands deep into the pockets of his jeans. "Public displays of affection are taboo as far as you're concerned?"

"We...we're adults," Shelby stammered. "Not a couple of... of hormonally driven teens. We can't maul each other in front of everyone. It's unseemly, to say the least."

"The problem is, you make me feel like a hormonally driven teen, Shelby. And I'm not sure what to do about it." He laughed slightly. "Except maybe to maul you, wherever we happen to be."

Garrett stood still as a stone, struggling to regain his usual iron control. When he'd touched her it was as if some internal switch had been flipped, freeing all his masculine urges, allowing him to actively pursue what he wanted and not stop until he got it. It was not unlike his pursuits in business, except this was personal, as personal as it could possibly be. He wanted Shelby Halford. He had an almost overpowering urge to pick her up and take her to some private, quiet place where he could slip off those little shorts she was wearing and sink himself deep inside her.

Shelby stared at him, noting the flush of his cheekbones, the sexual intensity burning in his dark blue eyes. It was the hard, hungry way men looked at Laney. No one had ever looked at her that way. What man would dare risk it? Her forbidding, icy demeanor sent men running like cockroaches after a blast of insecticide.

Except Garrett wasn't running. He'd already been subjected to her most forbidding iciness, nevertheless he was looking at her with undisguised sexual desire.

She dragged her eyes away from him. Her imagination was running away with her, she decided nervously. Perhaps it was the intense heat. If so, she wasn't the only one affected.

"I—I think the afternoon sun must be getting to you," she told him lightly, attempting to sound flippant. She might have succeeded but for the tremulous note in her voice. "I am not the type to drive a man to lust."

"Something else we disagree on. I'm a man and I can offer you irrefutable evidence of the lust you've inspired."

Involuntarily, her eyes dropped to the front of his jeans where the evidence was irrefutable indeed. Mortified, she quickly looked away, feeling a sharp surge of hot color stain her cheeks.

"Shall we take the tour?" Grinning wickedly, Garrett reached for her hand and walked her to the house.

The dark clouds grew nearer and the sea breezes grew stiffer, but Shelby and Garrett ignored them and continued their exploration of the town. Since this was his first trip, she suggested that he choose the sites that interested him. The ones he chose, the Historic Key West Shipwreck Museum and the Key West Hurricane Museum, happened to be places she'd never visited before.

She found both interesting, even engrossing, surprising herself. "I've always avoided those places," she confessed as they emerged into the light drizzle that had begun to fall. "I thought they'd only appeal to ghoulish voyeur types. You know, the kind who slow down at accident sites to get a better look. The group who enjoy watching videotapes of actual catastrophes."

"There you go again, generalizing and stereotyping," Garrett admonished lightly. "Sometimes you have to try to see things from a different angle, Shelby."

Shelby looked thoughtful. "The way that you do."

He laughed. "Some might argue that I see things from a warped angle."

"No, I'm serious, Garrett. You're always open to new information and ideas, asking questions, looking at everything, seeking answers."

"A veritable creative genius," he said drolly.

She knew he was kidding, but she wasn't. She admired him, Shelby realized with a jolt. It had nothing to do with the sexual chemistry between them, which was a separate and potent issue of its own. What she was feeling now went beyond physical attraction. She admired his mind and appreciated his talent and skills in the difficult and capricious hotel business. It was both stirring and stimulating to talk to him, to laugh with him and argue with him. Even just to be with him.

When was the last time she'd felt this way about a man? For that matter, when was the first time? She couldn't remember. She'd never felt this way before and it was happening so fast. Too fast. Shelby gazed at him, apprehension and excitement surging through her, so intermingled that she couldn't begin to separate one from the other. It was both scary and exhilarating. She felt so very vulnerable, she who had always prided herself on her invulnerability.

"I think we should head back to Port Key," she said firmly, moving carefully away from him.

Garrett noticed her withdrawal and it affected him in the most primally male way. He went after her, catching her by the hand. "I'd like to buy a few souvenirs first," he said, his voice as firm as hers. He drew her toward him, his fingers tightening around hers.

"Oh, no, not that awful place with the dead alligators again!" Shelby groaned. "Garrett, we have to leave. It's getting late. Look how dark the sky is. And it's starting to rain harder."

"I don't mind shopping in, shall we say, more upscale stores, if you'll show me where they are."

"There are some wonderful bookstores and galleries here," she said slowly, remembering them. "I haven't been in them for such a long time and I would like to see what's new."

"Well, then, lead the way." He held on to her hand, rubbing his thumb along her palm, stroking in a slow, sensuous rhythm.

Shelby felt a delicious warmth tighten and throb deeply, intimately, within her. Sensation blitzed her common sense and she found herself grinning when a big, heavy raindrop pelted her in the face. Her smile didn't fade as the rain began to fall heavier and faster, offering stark proof of her current dilemma.

How could she follow the most sensible, practical course and insist that Garrett take her home without further delay when she didn't even have the sense to come in out of the rain?

Six

"**Y**ou have remarkable stamina," Shelby told Garrett as they crowded under the umbrella they'd bought, clutching the bags filled with their purchases. "And you lay to rest the stereotype about men hating to shop." Rain splashed down, the wind blowing and spraying it on them, despite the umbrella.

"Living with a mother, grandmother and five sisters, my brothers and I learned to tolerate shopping. At least you didn't spend hours trying on clothes. Back in high school, my sister Gracie set the world record, which still stands in the McGrath family to this day—it took her four hours to find a white T-shirt.

"You, on the other hand, have a no-nonsense approach to clothes," Garrett continued drolly. "You don't mind being outfitted by Julio's Gifts and Sundries. And a fetching outfit it is," he added, surveying her shorts and shirt.

She eyed him archly. "Maybe I'll spend the next four hours looking for just that perfect white T."

"You wouldn't!" He feigned alarm.

Their comments on time caused Shelby to automatically check her watch. She received quite a shock. "Oh, my goodness, it's seven o'clock! I didn't realize it was so late."

"Time flies when you're having fun," Garrett reminded her.

And they had been having fun, Shelby silently agreed. It was as if they were on vacation together, a couple leisurely wiling away the hours, looking and sampling and buying the local wares.

And now the day had turned into evening. "We really have to leave," Shelby said decisively.

"If you say so. Shall we have dinner, though, before we set out for Port Key?" Garrett's voice was muffled by a loud crack of thunder.

Shelby glanced up at the sky just as a bolt of lightning flashed. "The storm seems to be getting worse."

A gust of wind tugged at the umbrella, almost blowing it inside out. Garrett held on to it fast. "The wind is picking up, too. Maybe we should postpone the drive back to Port Key until the morning. We'll have dinner and then head over to the—"

"We're going back to Port Key *tonight*," Shelby announced. It would be so easy to slip back into the vacationing couple fantasy; a romantic dinner for two would certainly prolong the idyll. Followed by a night at a motel that they both knew had only one available room. She gulped. "And we're leaving right now."

Visibility was terrible. The sky was as black as a moonless midnight and sheets of heavy rain swept across the road as thick as a curtain.

"This is like trying to drive through Niagara Falls," groaned Garrett as he steered the little red car slowly down the highway. It chugged gallantly along, although the wind rocked it with increasing force. The beams cast by the headlights were practically useless in the thick swirling mist. If there happened to be a car in front of them, they probably wouldn't see it until they'd run into the bumper.

"This is what I get for playing the gentleman and ceding to your wishes, against my better instincts," he lamented. "I knew we should've stayed in Key West tonight. I should have insisted, should have trusted my—"

"Please, no more about your infallible instincts," Shelby cut in exasperatedly. "You've been ranting on about them for miles. They obviously failed you this time or you would have simply refused to drive back tonight. When you're set on a course of action, nothing deters you, certainly nothing as paltry as my wishes. Our trip down here together is proof of that."

Garrett frowned. She was right, of course. That was as galling to admit as the failure of his heretofore infallible instincts.

They both lapsed into a grim silence.

Crossing the bridges in the tiny car was truly terrifying. The wind howled and the rain pelted the car from every direction. It felt as if they were suspended in space, enshrouded by the unbreakable expanse of darkness from sky to sea. The water was on all sides of them, the whitecaps growing higher and wilder, the only light to be seen. Back on land again, Garrett heaved a sigh of relief that Shelby silently seconded.

She sat, wired and tense, beside him. "During all the years I lived in Florida, I've never seen a storm come up as fast and as furious as this one." They noticed a few cars stopped alongside the road. Either they had stalled or, more likely, the drivers had decided to pull over and wait for the rain to subside.

But the rain was relentless, pounding the car with unnerving ferocity. Even at top speed, the windshield wipers couldn't clear the water away fast enough for adequate visibility. Garrett slowed the car to a crawl but kept on driving. Lightning bolts seemed to surround them, flashing in the sky in a spectacular light show. The accompanying claps of thunder were deafening. Shelby fought the childish urge to cover her ears with her hands to block out the sound.

They drove slowly on, passing yet another car on the narrow shoulder of the road. A fierce gust of wind sent the little car careening to the left and Garrett used all his strength to pull it back on course.

"This car is so tiny," Shelby whispered, her heart in her throat. "I'm afraid the wind will pick it up and toss it around like a beach ball."

Garrett was, too. But he wasn't about to admit it and further alarm her. "I wish my infallible instincts had instructed me to rent the agency's largest car instead of the smallest for this trip," he said wryly.

She couldn't help but smile. His self-mocking humor in the face of danger appealed to her and lightened the tension. "That old hearse you rented back in Kansas would come in handy about now," she agreed.

"We're still in the Lower Keys. I wonder how long it'll take to get to Halford House at this rate?"

"At the expeditious speed of an inch a minute? This drive could end up lasting longer than the Crusades." Shelby made another stab at humor, trying to fight the anxiety surging through her. Being scared in a thunderstorm, however torrential the rains and high the winds, was wimpy and weak, she scolded herself. And that's all it was, a severe thunderstorm, not the evil twin of horrific Hurricane Andrew.

Garrett fiddled with the radio, finally finding a station that could be heard above the roar of static blanketing the airwaves. As luck would have it, it was a Spanish-language station, with the music, commercials, and disc jockey patter entirely in Spanish. They listened for a while, hoping for an English word. The closest they got was Miami.

"How could you be born and raised in Florida, live here for seventeen years, and not know any Spanish?" Garrett complained.

"I took French in high school," Shelby mumbled. She felt inordinately stupid.

"And then you lived in California for the next ten years and managed not to learn any Spanish there, either." Garrett frowned his disapproval. "You've lived in two states with sizable Hispanic populations and yet you've—"

"All right, all right! You've made your point. I'm sure if *you'd* been in my position, you would've been fluent in Spanish by now. You would probably be working as a translator in your spare time."

His lips quirked. "Undoubtedly."

"Well, I'm signing up for one of those crash courses in Spanish as soon as possible. That is, if we aren't blown away or drowned in this storm," she added gloomily.

"We aren't going to be blown away or drowned. Everything is going to be all right, Shelby."

"You don't know that. You couldn't possibly know if things will turn out all right or end tragically. You admitted yesterday that you aren't psychic."

"True. But I am realistic," Garrett said calmly. "The odds of coming through this storm unscathed are very much in our favor."

Shelby sighed. "You're one of those indefatigable optimists, aren't you? The kind who looks at a glass of water and says it's half-full instead of half-empty."

"If I see a glass with water in it, I either drink it or pour it down the sink. I don't stand around contemplating it."

They drove over another bridge and the span seemed to sway and shake from the sheer force of the wind. Knowing that the turbulent waters of the Atlantic and the Gulf swirled wildly beneath them on either side, that the safety of land was a tentative distance in both directions, added a particularly perilous touch.

"This is enough to induce a lifelong phobia of bridges," Shelby said nervously, staring out the windshield. There was nothing to see but the fog in the surrounding darkness and the rain striking the glass.

Garrett glanced over at her. She was gnawing the knuckles of one hand while tightly clenching the other into a white-knuckled fist.

"The storm shows no signs of abating," he said quietly. "If anything, the rain seems to be coming down harder and the winds are gusting even higher. We're going to have to stop, Shelby. It would be stupid to try to cross the Seven Mile Bridge in this storm. Especially in this little car.''

Shelby thought of that bridge, the world's largest segmental bridge that spanned the broad expanse of water separating the Lower and Middle Keys. It was an awesome engineering feat and crossing it on a sunny day, when one could fully appreciate the combined effects of the scenery and the technology, was a high point of the drive along the Overseas Highway.

Then she imagined crossing the Seven Mile Bridge tonight with the wind and the rain and the black, churning waters serving as a frightening backdrop. Navigating the smaller bridges in this storm had been dire enough; the prospect of a seven-mile trek across the open seas was horrifying.

"Are you going to pull over and wait till the rain lets up?'' she murmured.

"Who knows when that'll be? An hour from now? Or in the middle of the night? We're still hours from Port Key, Shelby. We'll have to stop for the night at the first place we come to.''

Shelby protested immediately. It was understandable, even wise, to pull off the road and wait for the worst of the storm to pass. But she was *not* going to spend the night with him in a motel. She'd already refused to do so when the ingratiating Tony Fontana had offered them a free room at the Family Fun Inn. Her refusal still stood.

She was still arguing her case when Garrett pulled off the road, over to a dilapidated, single-story building of motel units sporting a hand-painted sign that read Seagull Motel. He stopped the car in front of the door that had Office printed on it in big block letters.

Shelby panicked. "I'm not setting foot in this place! Why, I've seen better-looking roach motels. And Norman Bates is probably the proprietor here.''

"You've seen *Psycho*?" Garrett sounded extraordinarily pleased. "I'm a rabid Hitchcock fan, I've seen every one of his films at least five times and—"

"Just because I've seen *Psycho* doesn't mean I care to live it. I—"

A bottle suddenly hit the windshield, hurled by the force of the wind. The bottle shattered, spewing glass, but fortunately the windshield was strong enough to withstand the assault and didn't even crack.

Garrett frowned grimly. "We're getting out of this car right now, Shelby. A concrete block or brick might come crashing through one of the windows and clobber us. Get your packages and come on."

"No!"

"I'll carry you inside if I have to," he warned. His blue eyes were flinty with determination. "If that's what you want, then just sit here and keep saying no."

"You can't bully me! I—"

He opened the door and a blast of wind and rain filled the car. "I'm going to get us a room. I'll be back for you."

A room, he'd said. Not two rooms. Shelby was instantly galvanized into action. "I demand my own room!" she called after him. "If we have to stay here, we're renting two rooms." She tumbled out of the car, slamming the door behind her. The wind was so strong, it almost knocked her off her feet.

Garrett returned to grab her and, holding tightly to her, they battled the wind to trudge the few feet into the dimly lit office of the Seagull Motel.

Stepping inside, they learned the reason why the office was so dimly lit. The power was out and the only illumination came from several candles that were burning on top of the desk. A pudgy, red-haired clerk sat behind it, eating from an open bag of pork rinds and listening to the radio.

"Hello there, folks!" he greeted them jovially. "Got caught in the storm, huh? It's a bad one. Close to hurricane-force winds, the weather report says. Caught everybody by surprise."

"See? Not Norman Bates," Garrett whispered reassuringly to Shelby, out of earshot of the clerk.

Shelby glanced around the office whose seedy aura was apparent despite the lack of lights. The place was downright creepy. It wouldn't have surprised her to spot a mummified corpse reposing in a corner, most likely surrounded by a collection of dead baby alligators dressed in doll-size clothes.

"We'd like two rooms for the night please," Garrett said.

"Oh, I'm sorry, sir. We only have one room left," the clerk replied.

"What?" Shelby whirled around to face Garrett. She heard the hammer of her heartbeat echo in her ears. Suddenly her pulses were racing out of control.

Garrett watched her closely, taking in the rush of color to her cheeks, the rapid rise and fall of her breasts beneath the pink cotton of her shirt. He could feel the tension emanating from her, see it in the faint trembling of her body. Miss Halford was quite disturbed over the prospect of sharing a room with him. He found her overreaction amusing. Did she expect he would jump her the moment they were alone in a bedroom together? Or was she afraid that she might be tempted to jump him? Now there was an appealing notion!

"I said we only have one room available," the clerk replied.

"That means we have to share, Shelby," Garrett drawled.

"Place started filling up when the storm got bad. Travelers like yourself pulling over," the clerk explained, sounding thrilled. "We haven't had full occupancy since 1974. Kind of a historic night for us here at the Seagull."

"Well, we can't stay," Shelby said frantically. Her heart was pounding in a painful panic and her eyes compulsively slid over Garrett's long, lean length, from his powerful shoulders to his flat belly. She quickly jerked her gaze away. "We need two rooms. We'll drive on until we find—"

"We're staying." Garrett's tone brooked no argument. "We're not going to risk being out in the storm in a car that's as big as a dessert cart. We'll take the room," he added decisively.

"The power's out and we don't know when it'll be restored," the clerk warned. "But we're still charging the regular rate. Payable in advance."

"Forty-five dollars for this dump!" an indignant Garrett exclaimed a short while later. He was pacing the last room available at the Seagull Motel. "What an outrage!"

He gestured toward the double bed, its lumpy mattress and threadbare spread apparent even in the flickering light provided by one of the two candles the clerk had given them. "Why, there's not even a TV set."

"Not that it matters," Shelby said glumly. "There's no electricity tonight. No lights, no air-conditioning, no air!" She cracked the door to let some fresh air inside. A blast of wind and rain swept in. Shelby surrendered to the inevitable and closed the door again. She turned her attention back to Garrett, who continued to pace like a restless tiger trapped in a too-small cage.

In addition to the bed, there was an old armchair and a nicked and scratched three-drawer bureau squeezed into the room, leaving only a narrow strip between the door and the wall for pacing. There was also a bathroom the size of a phone booth.

"We could always leave," she suggested hopefully. "We don't have to stay here. There have to be other places farther along the—"

"We don't have a choice. You heard what the guy said— hurricane-force winds. We're not going to drive through them. We're here and we're going to make the best of it." Garrett smiled grimly. "Actually, this is a good lesson for me. I can experience firsthand how and why Family Fun Inns have been so successful. With places like the Seagull Motel as our competition for low-budget rooms, no wonder business is booming. But we must never lose our edge and grow complacent."

"I appreciate your consumer-and-marketing lesson, but this place is truly awful, Garrett! How are we ever going to get through the whole night here? It's not quite ten o'clock yet. And I don't want to even touch that bedspread, let alone sit on it."

Garrett whipped the ancient spread off the bed. "The sheets are clean, they're actually starched," he noted, sliding his hands over the top sheet. "You can safely sit down, Shelby." He caught her hand. "Relax, honey. It's—"

"If you're about to make a pass, you can save yourself the effort," she said trenchantly. "You don't have a prayer of seducing me in a rattletrap like this, so don't even try."

Garrett grinned. "Setting is important to you, hmm? Candlelight, wine, soft music."

"A bed that doesn't look like someone died in it. A room that doesn't reek of must and mildew. Call me finicky, but those are my minimal requirements."

He carried her hand to his lips and kissed her fingertips. "How about if I call you discerning. Particular. A discriminating woman with fastidious tastes. And, no, this is not a pass. Give me credit for a little style, Shelby. I certainly wouldn't want to consummate our relationship in a rat hole like the Seagull Motel."

Her heart lurched and she snatched her hand away from him. "We're not going to *consummate* our relationship anywhere, Garrett McGrath. We don't even have a relationship."

"Don't we?"

"Certainly not!" she insisted swiftly and forcefully. Too swiftly and too forcefully, she realized at once. It would've been so much more effective to simply smile and shrug off his light remark with a sophisticated, casual reply of her own.

Her eyes narrowed with displeasure and she glared at him. "And don't you dare try to come back with that overused quotation about the 'lady doth protest too much'!"

"I don't have to. You're doing an excellent job of it all on your own."

"An excellent job of what?" she snapped.

"Of verifying that we do indeed have a relationship. One that most certainly will be consummated. In time. But not tonight."

Even in the darkness, she could see the devilish gleam in his eyes. He was teasing her. Baiting her. And she'd fallen right into the trap. She flopped down on the edge of the bed and stared at the candle, their only source of light. It was burning quickly, melted wax running down the sides as the flame flickered.

"When this candle burns down, we can light the other one, but what happens when it goes out, too?" she mused nervously.

"Then we're totally in the dark. The clerk was very definite about the two-candles-per-room limit." Garrett sat down beside her on the bed. "Are you hungry?"

She nodded. "It's been a long time since lunch. Too bad we didn't eat dinner before we left Key West."

"This seems to be the ideal time to mention that I suggested having dinner before setting out on this drive from hell. I also suggested not making the drive at all tonight. Sharing a room at a Family Fun Inn beats a night at the Seagull hands down."

"But then you would've missed this marvelous learning opportunity provided by the Seagull." There was a taunting gleam in her hazel eyes.

"Touché." Garrett grinned. He reached for the bags he'd set down on the armchair, which were filled with his purchases from Key West. "Don't worry, we're not going to starve tonight. While you were in that card shop, I bought some souvenir food to bring home to the family. But since we're both hungry, we might as well eat it now."

"Souvenir food?" Shelby echoed. "I'm almost afraid to ask what that is."

"It's stuff that's indigenous to the area, interesting things to eat that you probably won't find in Buffalo." Garrett pulled the items from the bags. "Like Key lime saltwater taffy. A jar of papaya, banana and pineapple in cinnamon and currant jelly sauce. Guava fudge. Lychee nuts. Here, help yourself."

Shelby declined. "On second thought, maybe I'd rather starve tonight."

Garrett shrugged, unwrapped a piece of taffy and popped it in his mouth. "I've tasted worse," was all he said, hardly a glowing endorsement. "I also bought some souvenir beverages," he added, handing Shelby another bag.

She pulled out a decanter shaped like a mermaid and read the label. "Circe's Spiced Rum." There was another, traditional-shaped bottle inside the bag, as well. "Captain Jolly's Lime-flavored Rum." She shuddered. "These are evil-looking brews. The lime rum is tinted green!"

"I thought Gran could break it open next St. Patrick's Day." Garrett sampled the fudge and coughed. "Well, the fudge gets a thumbs down from me. Try a bite." He held a piece of it to her lips.

Shelby took a hamster-size nibble and grimaced. "Ugh! Make that two thumbs down."

Garrett tossed the partially eaten piece of fudge into the wastebasket in the corner. "Two points," he explained when it hit. "I haven't lost my touch."

"Did you play basketball?"

He nodded. "In high school and college. I wasn't bad but I wasn't great, either. The sport didn't lose a potential superstar when I gave it up."

"So what sport do you play now?" she asked. "Golf?"

"I've picked up a golf club on occasion."

She made a muffled sound and looked away.

"Are you snickering at me behind my back?" He snatched her ponytail and tugged on it, forcing her to look at him. "Aha, you are!"

"I'm just trying to picture you on the golf course, playing a few rounds with the exalted captains of the hotel industry. I bet you caused some brows to arch when you showed up in your jeans and Niagara Falls Is For Lovers T-shirt."

"Would you snicker if I told you about my madras golf slacks and peacock blue golf shirt?"

"The mind reels." She did snicker again, she couldn't help herself.

Another piece of fudge thudded into the wastebasket. "Slam dunk," he proclaimed. "Care to give it a shot?"

While Shelby was taking aim with a piece of taffy, he twisted open the cap on the bottle of Circe's Spiced Rum and took a swallow of the dark brown liquid. "Whew!" He shook his head, as if to clear it. "Circe packs one helluva punch."

Shelby's taffy landed several feet short of the wastebasket. She retrieved it and tried again. And missed again. Garrett made another perfect shot. Shelby missed once more.

"Your aim is pretty pathetic. Maybe Circe here can help you." He handed her the mermaid-shaped bottle.

"Are you trying to get me drunk?" she demanded suspiciously.

"So I can have my wicked way with you? Sorry to disappoint you, honey, but I do have my standards. And a seduction at the Seagull doesn't measure up to them."

"What does?" She put the bottle to her lips and took a tentative sip. Circe's Spiced Rum was fiery but surprisingly sweet, tasting more like soda pop than alcohol. She took a larger gulp this time. "What meets your exalted standards for seduction, anyway?"

Garrett took the bottle and drank from it. "There should be good food. Not too rich or too heavy. Or too sweet."

"That leaves out guava fudge and Key lime taffy," Shelby observed. She got the bottle back. The more she drank of this stuff, the better she liked it.

He nodded in agreement. "Maybe some fine wine. A nice California Chardonnay. Or maybe something French."

"That excludes Circe's Spiced Rum." She handed him the bottle. Her head was beginning to spin a little.

"A big, comfortable room with a beautiful view and an excellent mattress on the bed," he continued.

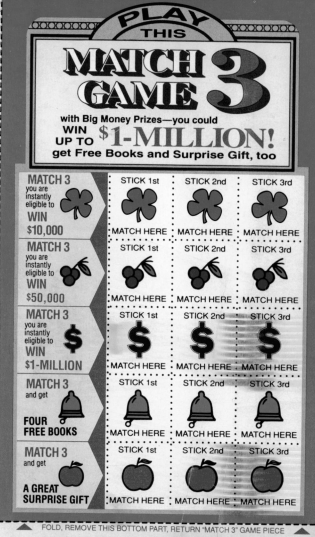

PLAY THIS MATCH GAME 3

with Big Money Prizes—you could WIN UP TO **$1-MILLION!**
get Free Books and Surprise Gift, too

MATCH 3 you are instantly eligible to WIN $10,000

STICK 1st	STICK 2nd	STICK 3rd
MATCH HERE	MATCH HERE	MATCH HERE

MATCH 3 you are instantly eligible to WIN $50,000

STICK 1st	STICK 2nd	STICK 3rd
MATCH HERE	MATCH HERE	MATCH HERE

MATCH 3 you are instantly eligible to WIN $1-MILLION

STICK 1st	STICK 2nd	STICK 3rd
MATCH HERE	MATCH HERE	MATCH HERE

MATCH 3 and get **FOUR FREE BOOKS**

STICK 1st	STICK 2nd	STICK 3rd
MATCH HERE	MATCH HERE	MATCH HERE

MATCH 3 and get **A GREAT SURPRISE GIFT**

STICK 1st	STICK 2nd	STICK 3rd
MATCH HERE	MATCH HERE	MATCH HERE

FOLD, REMOVE THIS BOTTOM PART, RETURN "MATCH 3" GAME PIECE

THIS COULD BE THE LUCKIEST DAY OF YOUR LIFE

because your "MATCH 3" Game qualifies you for a chance to win a Big Money Prize—up to $1-MILLION in Lifetime Cash—for FREE! It's also your chance to get Free Books & an Exciting Free Surprise Gift with no obligation to buy anything, now or ever. Just find all the matching stamps you can, stick them on your Game, fill in your name & address on the other side & return your Game in the reply envelope provided. We'll take care of the rest!

HERE'S HOW TO PLAY
"MATCH 3"

1 Detach this, your "MATCH 3" Game, & the page of stamps enclosed. Look for matching symbols among the stamps & stick all you find on your "MATCH 3" Game.

2 Successfully complete rows 1 through 3 & you will instantly & automatically qualify for a chance to win a Big Money Prize—up to a MILLION-$$$ in Lifetime Income ($33,333.33 each year for 30 years). (SEE BACK OF BOOK FOR DETAILS.)

3 Successfully complete row 4 & we will send you 4 brand-new SIILHOUETTE DESIRE® novels—for FREE! These Free Books have a cover price of $2.99 each, but they are yours to keep absolutely free. There's no catch. You're under no obligation to buy anything. We charge nothing—ZERO—for your first shipment. And you don't have to make any minimum number of purchases—not even one!

4 The fact is, thousands of Readers enjoy receiving books by mail from the Silhouette Reader Service®. They like the convenience of home delivery...they like getting the best new novels months before they're available in stores...and they love our discount prices!

5 Successfully complete row 5 &, in addition to the Free Books, we will also send you a very nice Free Surprise Gift, as extra thanks for trying our Reader Service.

6 Play the "Lucky Stars" & "Dream Car TieBreaker" Games also enclosed & you could WIN AGAIN & AGAIN because these are Bonus Prizes, all for one winner, & on top of any Cash Prize you may win!

YES! I've completed my "MATCH 3" Game. Send me any Big Money Prize to which I am entitled just as soon as winners are determined. Also send me the Free Books & Free Surprise Gift under the no-obligation-to-buy-ever terms explained above and on the back of the stamps & reply. (No purchase necessary as explained below.)

225 CIS AQXC
(U-SIL-D-09/94)

Name

Street Address   Apt. #

City   State   Zip Code
©1991 HARLEQUIN ENTERPRISES LTD.

LUCKY STARS

Everybody's got a Lucky Star & this may be yours. SCRATCH GOLD FROM BOX & STAR. You're* definitely in — you qualify for a chance to win the Super Bonus Prize revealed.

HAWAII 2 WEEKS FOR 2

HAWAII 2 WEEKS FOR 2

PRE-FOLD BONUS GAMES & SEPARATE AT DOTTED LINES — PL

Extra EXTRA

Super DOUBLE BONUS PRIZE

Prizes on these Games are BONUS EXTRAS, all for 1 winner, AND on top of

Use These Stamps to Complete Your
"MATCH 3" Game

Simply detach this page & see how many matches you can find for your "MATCH 3" Game. Then take the matching stamps and stick them on the Game. Three-of-a-kind matches in rows 1 through 3 qualify you for a chance to win a Big Money Prize—up to a Million-$$$ ...

...THREE-OF-A-KIND-MATCHES IN ROWS 4 & 5 GETS YOU FREE BOOKS & A NICE SURPRISE GIFT AS WELL! PLAYING IS FREE - FUN - EASY & THE WAY YOU COULD WIN!

PLAY TODAY!

PLAY "MATCH 3" –YOU COULD WIN UP TO A MILLION-$$$ IN LIFETIME INCOME (YES, $1,000,000!) –GET FREE BOOKS & AN EXCITING SURPRISE GIFT, TOO!

★ Did you complete the first 3 rows of your "Match 3" Game? Did you print your name & address on the Game? Are you also playing & enclosing your Bonus Games? Please do, because so doing definitely qualifies you for a chance to win one of the Fabulous Prizes being offered, up to & including a MILLION-$$$ in Lifetime Income!

★ Did you complete rows 4 & 5? If you did, you are entitled to Free Books & a really nice Surprise Gift, as your introduction to our Reader Service. The Service does not require you to buy ever. When you get your Free Books, if you don't want any more, just write cancel on the statement & return it to us.

★ You can of course go for prizes alone by not playing rows 4 & 5. But why pass up such good things? Why not go for all the prizes you can - & why not get everything that's being offered & that you're entitled to? It's all free, yours to keep & enjoy. It's a "SURE FIRE" opportunity for you!

She ran her hand over a spring in the lump mattress. "Things being how they are, the Seagull is definitely out of the running for 'ideal setting.'" Somehow the bottle was back in her hands. She automatically drank from it.

"Romantic music playing in the background," Garrett added.

"Without electricity, nothing is playing in the background here except what is provided by Mother Nature. Would you classify the sound of debris hitting the window as romantic?"

"And most important of all, I have to be with the right woman. That would make it a mutual seduction, with her wanting me as much as I want her. Which isn't seduction at all, but making love."

Shelby took another swig of spiced rum. "And how often does this happen? You finding yourself with Ms. Right in the ideal setting with the perfect food, wine and music? Once a week? Twice? Every night?"

"I'm not a womanizer, Shelby, if that's what you're asking."

"Whether you are or you aren't doesn't matter to me. How you choose to entertain yourself in your spare time doesn't interest me in the slightest." This time she scored a direct hit with the taffy into the wastebasket.

"Hmm, what was it you said earlier, about the lady doth protest too much?"

"I didn't say it. I warned *you* not to say it."

"Ah. Well, now that we've cleared that up, would you care to sample some of Captain Jolly's potion?"

"Absolutely not! I don't drink anything that's green, and you shouldn't, either."

"I think we're on to something here." Garrett snapped his fingers. "Both green doors and green liquids lack popular appeal."

"Quick, call market research!"

They both laughed. And passed the bottle of Circe's Spiced Rum. And aimed more pieces of candy into the wastebasket.

Seven

Bright rays of sunshine streamed through the slats of the dingy old venetian blinds, flooding the small motel room with light. Shelby stirred and cracked open one eye. She was lying flat on her back on the bed in a shabby, dilapidated room with water stains zigzagging across the ceiling. Outside, the sounds of howling wind and teeming rain were conspicuously absent.

Shelby stirred, feeling unpleasantly sticky in the hot, stuffy room. She was still wearing the shorts and shirt Garrett had bought her yesterday. For the first time in her life she'd gone to bed in her clothes, without faithfully completing her normal nightly ablutions.

He lay beside her, fully dressed and sound asleep, facing her. Shelby allowed her gaze to linger on him, sweeping over the sharp features of his face. With those alert and assessing blue eyes of his closed, she was able to study him at her leisure, and she took full advantage. The firm line of his mouth, his lips, well-defined and sensuous, were particularly compelling. His strong jaw, usually smooth and close-shaven, was now darkened with stubble. Fascinated, she almost reached out to touch it, but she restrained herself. She didn't want to awaken him; she wasn't quite ready to face him yet.

Shelby sat up abruptly and stifled a moan. She felt as if she'd taken a sharp jab to the head. She gazed around, focusing on the scene around her. Candy and wrappers littered the floor, the wastebasket was overturned, and an empty mermaid-shaped bottle sat on top of the ugly old bureau. The moldy, musty smell of mildew assailed her nostrils when she took a deep breath.

It was the morning-after a riotous night-before at the Seagull Motel.

"What time is it?" Garrett mumbled, keeping his eyes tightly closed.

Shelby glanced at her watch. "Quarter to eight. It's stopped raining," she added unnecessarily. Now that the opening remarks were out of the way, she felt herself begin to relax a little.

"You didn't by any chance take a mallet and pound me over the head with it last night, did you?" Garrett tentatively touched his temples with his fingertips and grimaced.

"Not unless you did the same to me and neither of us remembers." Shelby began to gingerly rub her scalp. "I think it's more than likely that our old friend Circe is to blame."

Garrett rolled over onto his stomach, resting his head on his arms. "She's one potent siren. Now I know how all those hapless sailors met their doom. If I'd been steering a boat last night under Circe's influence, I'd have ended up crashing on the rocks for sure. You don't happen to have any aspirin with you, do you?"

"As a matter of fact, I do." Shelby slowly climbed out of bed and fumbled for her purse. She took two pills herself, before ministering to Garrett.

"You're an angel of mercy." He sat up to gratefully swallow the medicine and drain the water glass dry. "This room is even worse than I imagined it last night in the dark," he murmured, looking around. His eyes flicked over the candy and overturned wastebasket. "The tournament," he recalled. "I won, I believe."

"That remains undecided. After both candles burned out, it was too dark to tell if the candy hit the wastebasket or missed it. You claimed every single one of your shots hit, but I know they didn't."

"Yes, they did. All those pieces of candy lying around are your misses. And am I delirious or did we actually sing the theme songs of every movie and TV show we could think of last night?"

"When we didn't know the words, we hummed the tune," she confirmed. "I think we were both, uh, slightly juiced at that point."

"I remember looking at my watch and having trouble focusing on the numbers glowing in the dark. It was almost four o'clock. After that, it's oblivion."

"I was all ready for another round of 'Name That Tune,' but you sort of keeled over and went to sleep," said Shelby. "Just like a man," she added with a wicked superior grin.

"What an unforgivable breach of etiquette! I promise that the next night you spend in bed with me, I won't roll over and go to sleep until you're fully satisfied."

"Promises, promises," she joked.

She was pleased that they'd easily resumed the camaraderie they had developed during last night's stormy siege. She even enjoyed his suggestive teasing in a way she'd previously been unable to, before they'd logged so many hours together.

Garrett swung his legs over the side of the bed and groaned. "I'd kill for a long, hot shower, a razor and a toothbrush and a change of clothes."

"Wait until you see the bathroom in the light. There's mold that looks like it dates back to prehistoric times," Shelby warned, walking into the bathroom to look around. "This shower could qualify as a scientific experiment."

"Then maybe we should forgo that dubious pleasure and head straight back to Port Key. Do you feel up to resuming our journey?"

Shelby caught a glimpse of herself in the mirror over the sink and grimaced. Her hair hung loose and straight around her shoulders and her bangs were askew. Her clothes, cheap and wrinkled, looked as if she'd slept in them, which of course, she had. "I could be the poster girl for grunge. Are you sure you want to be seen traveling with me?"

Garrett came to stand behind her and wrapped his arms around her waist. He nuzzled her hair away and kissed the soft, slender column of her neck. "You look pretty damn good to me," he said huskily.

His nearness, his smoldering sexuality, hit her with the force of a sledgehammer. She was suddenly breathless and had to fight the urge to lean back into him, to rest her head in the hollow of his shoulder. He trailed a path of tiny, stinging kisses along her neck while his fingers kneaded the soft swell of her belly.

He met her eyes in the mirror. "If I had to be stuck in the Seagull Motel for a night, there's nobody I'd have rather been with than you."

"I think that's what is called a backhanded compliment." Shelby laughed shakily. Her knees felt rubbery. She could feel the heat of his hard body burning through her, could feel the strength of him in the big warm hands that were lightly caressing her. His arousal throbbed potently against her, an unmistakable reminder of his virility. And of his desire... for her. Shelby trembled.

"Not backhand at all." Garrett turned her carefully in his arms to face him, molding her against him, stroking her closer until she melted into him. Then his mouth touched hers gently, brushing her lips with his, back and forth, in a slow, seductive rhythm.

Shelby held her breath, desire twisting sharply through her. The sensual effects evoked by his caresses were strong and instant. Her breasts tingled and ached as her nipples tightened, and a sweet, hot tension gripped her loins.

"Next time we spend a night together, we won't pass the time playing singing games and shooting pieces of candy into the trash can. Not that I didn't have a great time with you last night.'' His mouth was touching hers as he spoke, and she shivered with sensual arousal. ''I have a great time with you no matter where we are or what we're doing.''

His words sent a flood of warmth surging through her. It was the first time she'd ever heard such a sentiment expressed to her or about her. Shelby was well aware that spending time with her didn't exactly qualify as anybody's idea of fun. From the time she'd been a very little girl, she had known that Laney was the child of choice; the prickly, defensive shell she'd built around herself didn't inspire others to look to her for fun, laughs, and good times, either. Yet here was Garrett McGrath telling her that he liked being with her.

''No matter how awful the setting or trying the circumstances?'' she queried lightly.

''It doesn't get much worse than a night without electricity in the Seagull Motel and I'd do it again tonight if you'd be here with me.''

He cupped her face with one hand, gently caressing the soft skin of her cheek with his fingertips, his thumb tracing the fine line of her jaw. He used his other hand to settle her intimately against him.

Shelby felt the hard bulge of his sex pressing insistently against her own yielding softness and a fiery ache burned and throbbed within her, spreading from that one erotic point of contact to every nerve and muscle of her body. She gazed helplessly into his eyes, drowning in their passionate blue depths, until she could no longer hold open her lids. They snapped shut as her mind seemed to short-circuit, sending her spinning into a world of pure sensation.

Garrett took her mouth again, this time with urgent and insistent demand. Eagerly, she parted her lips to the probing caress of his tongue and met it with her own.

The kiss was hot and deep, the sheer carnality of it staggering and addictive. Neither could bear to pull away, not even to breathe, so the kiss went on and on and on. When they were finally forced to break apart by sheer necessity, both were gulping for air. They stared at each other with glazed eyes, both breathing heavily.

For the first time in living memory, Garrett found himself at a loss for words. There was no easy quip that sprang quickly to his lips, no casual one-liner to lighten the atmosphere and put the kiss into perspective. Not that he knew what that perspective might be. The truth was, he'd never been so deeply and wildly affected by a kiss. Even their temperature-raising first kiss, which they'd shared in the ocean, hadn't packed the emotional wallop of this one.

He knew why, of course. It was because his emotions were involved, because the chemistry between them had been supplemented by the feelings he'd developed for her after their many hours together. He liked her, he enjoyed her company, even when she was sniping at him and challenging him. The McGraths didn't take to fawning sycophants, and the women he usually met who submissively pandered to his ego tended to bore him. No one could ever accuse Shelby Halford of pandering.

Garrett's lips curved into a smile. He couldn't imagine her boring him, either. Maddening him, perhaps, but that was all right. He'd lived his life among the maddening McGraths. He was one himself and proud of it.

Shelby stared at him, saw the secret smile twist his mouth and light his eyes. Her first reaction was to bristle in defense. All her old insecurities screamed that he was laughing at her, that she was the brunt of his own private joke. But before she dissolved into hurt and lashed out at him, a kinder, gentler, more optimistic point of view prevailed. One nurtured by what he'd told her earlier.

I have a great time with you no matter where we are or what we're doing.... It doesn't get much worse than a night without electricity in the Seagull Motel and I'd do it again tonight if you'd be here with me.

His words echoed in her head. He'd said them and then kissed her with a hungry, ardent passion that she had never before experienced. Buoyed by that knowledge, Shelby allowed herself to believe that maybe—just maybe—his smile was one of gladness, not derision. That maybe he felt the same excitement and anticipation that was joyously coursing through her. It was certainly powerful enough to make anyone smile.

They stopped at the first fast-food restaurant they saw, ordering from the drive-through window because neither cared to go inside. After the food was handed to them, Garrett pulled the little car into a parking space in the lot, where they ate their breakfast.

"This is the first time I've ever eaten one of these," Shelby remarked, taking a bite of a biscuit stuffed with an egg, sausage and cheese. "I normally have a piece of fruit, a bowl of hot cereal, and a cup of coffee for breakfast."

"You eat the same thing every day?"

"Well, the fruit is whatever happens to be in season, and I alternate between oatmeal and Cream of Wheat." She glanced over at him. He was unshaven and sweaty and wrinkled, but looked incredibly sexy in a disreputable sort of way. She remembered lying in bed next to him, waking up and staring at him as he slept.

A flame of sensual fire licked through her and she had to stop and think hard to regain her train of thought. They'd been talking about breakfast and her boring habit of never deviating from her fixed menu. She made a valiant attempt to continue the conversation. "I guess you vary your breakfasts the way you vary your rental cars and stay in rooms with different-colored doors."

"Variety is the spice of life," he affirmed. "Have you ever considered going nuts, throwing caution to the wind and having a bowl of cornflakes instead of the requisite hot cereal? Or being a complete rebel and opting for a Danish? Too crazy for you, huh?"

Shelby swallowed a bite of hash brown potato, another breakfast first for her. "Sometimes I think I may be a bit too regimented," she admitted slowly. "That I need to vary my routine a little."

"A lot," Garrett amended. "But you're off to a good start. And I intend to see to it that you continue."

"You do?"

"Mmm-hmm. I'm going to stick to you like gum on a shoe while I'm at Halford House. And every day is going to be different."

"And then you'll go back to Family Fun Inns' corporate headquarters in Buffalo and I'll take over running Halford House." She tried to keep her voice light and breezy but her spirits were drooping. She'd just stated the obvious and it hurt to hear it. Garrett's presence in her life was only temporary, a fact to keep in mind. Always.

But for the first time in her life, she understood how easy it would be to throw caution aside and simply get carried away by feelings, to stop thinking about tomorrow and live for the moment. To have a hot, no-strings affair with Garrett and damn the consequences. . . .

Except the consequences would undoubtedly end up damning her. Suddenly edgy and skittish, Shelby quickly retreated into her self-protective shell, where she was safe and solitary and in control of foolish impulses. She had no intention of being left a poor heartbroken fool, crying the blues when Garrett McGrath headed out of town.

Shelby's mention of herself running Halford House sent a sharp pang of consternation through Garrett. Last night's isolation in the storm had provided a respite from his deception dilemma, but this morning's sunshine and subsequent return to Halford House offered no similar escape. Or solution to the problem. They were no closer to the truth; Shelby still thought he'd purchased the Blue Springs Resort and was hanging around Halford House to learn the high-end of the hotel business.

The idea struck him as more and more preposterous, especially after getting to know Arthur Halford. Shelby, of all people, should realize that her father did not have a generous bone in his body. Art would no sooner let a budget-motel executive bunk in at Halford House to learn the ropes than he would spend a night behind a fuchsia door at a

Family Fun Inn. But then, Shelby didn't think her father would sell Halford House out from under her, either. She had seriously underestimated her father's cold-blooded, heartless quotient. When she learned the truth...

Garrett felt a mixture of sadness and concern for her. She would be crushed, but he vowed he would ease her pain. That is, if she let him. And that depended on how and when she learned the truth about the sale of Halford House and its buyer.

They were both quiet for the remainder of the drive to Port Key, preoccupied with their own thoughts and fighting the mounting fatigue resulting from their lack of sleep last night at the Seagull.

When they arrived back at the Halford House complex, Garrett dropped Shelby off at her parents' house, a small but comfortable ranch-style home on the perimeter of the grounds. She'd grown up there and upon her return from California had been ensconced back in her old bedroom, which had been stripped of all her old memorabilia and redecorated in the style of a Halford House guest room, in Halford green and ivory. Though she would have preferred one of the tiny bungalows set aside for upper management or even one of the staff rooms in the hotel annex, her parents had been insistent. She must stay in the family home. End of discussion.

Shelby had the car door open before Garrett braked to a full stop, and she hopped out the second he did. "Goodbye," she called over her shoulder, half running up the walk of inlaid stone.

Garrett recognized an escape when he saw one. He leaned out of the car and stood up, towering over the tiny red roof, to shout after her, "I'll see you later."

Her heart lurched. "No, I'm going to be very busy," she called back. She wasn't going to meekly acquiesce as he launched the fling that would break her heart. "I don't have time to see you."

Shelby fumbled with her key in the lock, willing the door to open immediately, just in case Garrett decided to follow her into the house. When he drove away toward cottage 101 instead, she told herself she was glad.

And knew she was lying. What she really was, was a seething mass of ambivalence, disappointed yet relieved that Garrett hadn't chased her into her home. Well, why should he? He thought he had plenty of time to woo her into his bed. He'd already tipped his hand earlier with his "I'm going to stick to you like gum on a shoe while I'm at Halford House" remark.

Ugh, gum on a shoe, she scorned. How disgusting and antiromantic! However, the operative phrase, the one that had set off her every defense, was the insouciant "while I'm at Halford House."

Tears of fury and exhaustion filled her eyes. So Garrett intended to have an affair with her for the duration of his visit and then fly north, leaving her behind without a second thought? Her temper flared. "Like hell he will!" she said aloud.

"Oh, you're back." Laney's appearance in the bright, airy foyer did nothing to improve Shelby's ever-worsening mood. As usual, Laney was impeccably dressed and made-up, her lustrous dark hair shiny, clean and perfectly coiffed. When she got a good look at bedraggled, Seagull-worn Shelby, her gorgeous eyes widened with horror. "What in the world happened to you?"

"We got stranded in the storm and had to spend the night in a dumpy motel in the Lower Keys." Shelby self-consciously tried to smooth her hair, then gave it up as hopeless. She knew she must look like something that had crawled out from under a rock.

Laney clearly thought so. She stared at her sister, appalled. "You and Garrett were stranded together in a motel?" she repeated incredulously.

"Nothing happened," Shelby was quick to reassure her. She cursed the ridiculous fiery blush that stained her cheeks.

"I should think not!" Laney laughed. "Not with you looking like that! And those clothes! They're worse than dreadful, Shelby. Where did you find them, in a trash container?''

Shelby wasn't up for explaining. An outfit from Julio's Gifts and Sundries probably equaled a Dumpster in Laney's mind, anyway. "It's a new look, called Dumpster chic. I take it you don't like it?"

Laney rolled her eyes. "May I give you some sisterly advice, Shelby? Take a shower and wash your hair, then burn those clothes. If you need something to wear, you can borrow something of mine. I seriously advise taking me up on my offer. Your own taste is—" She broke off, unable to come up with just the right derogatory term. "Well, I'm off to play tennis with Paul. Later, he's taking me to Miami Beach for dinner." She named an exclusive and very expensive restaurant there.

It occurred to Shelby that Paul, who had never even bought her a slice of pizza, was taking Laney to a place whose patrons' incomes and life-styles far exceeded his own. But then, Laney had a talent for inspiring men to treat her like the princess she fancied herself to be, even when they couldn't afford it.

Shelby tried to picture Laney's reaction to a night at the Seagull Motel and breakfast in a parking lot. Shelby gave up. It was too great a stretch for her imagination, anyway.

"Paul is a sweetie, and he's crazy about me. I hope you don't mind, Shel," Laney exclaimed breathlessly. "Paul and I didn't mean to fall in love and cut you out, but we were simply overwhelmed by our feelings. It was love at first sight for both of us." She shrugged and smiled artlessly.

"I don't feel at all slighted." Shelby's smile was equally artless. "Paul and I were co-workers and then friends, but we were never in love." Was that a shadow of disappointment that crossed Laney's lovely face? How vexing for Laney to realize that she'd snagged merely her sister's friend, not her lover, Shelby thought wryly.

"Anyway, I understand how it feels to have love strike like a lightning bolt." Shelby smiled with blinding sweetness. "It was that way for Garrett and me." With that, she sauntered down the hall to her own room, Laney's indignant gasp echoing in her ears.

Firing that volley was a measure of how exhausted she really was, Shelby decided, and conceded that a certain orneriness was involved, as well. Not to mention humor. *Love strike like a lightning bolt?* She almost laughed aloud at the hyperbole, but knew her sister hadn't found it funny. She'd deliberately incited Laney because from Laney's point of view, a man who fell for Shelby instead of her was committing an act of treason.

Shelby stripped and stepped gratefully under the hot, revitalizing spray of the shower. *Love at first sight for her and Garrett! Ha!* She really should be ashamed of herself for telling Laney such a whopper. But she felt no shame, not even a little. Instead, she felt a wistful longing that she quickly sought to suppress.

She did *not* wish that she and Garrett really had fallen in love at first sight. And she hadn't been struck by any love-tinged lightning bolts, either.

Garrett couldn't remember the last time he'd appreciated the simple joys of a hot shower as much as this one in the luxury bathroom of cottage 101. He was also enjoying the more luxurious pleasures as a guest—and *owner*—of Halford House. He padded into the living room wrapped in the thick, white, terry robe provided by the hotel, its crest embroidered on the front in Halford green thread.

The cottage was perfectly temperature controlled, dispelling the heat and humidity without resorting to the cryptlike frigidity that air-conditioning sometimes inflicted. He helped himself to some of the fresh fruit arranged in a bowl in the small kitchenette, then opened the refrigerator to find it stocked with everything from soda pop to fruit juice to imported beer to bottles of designer water. He was about to make his selection when a knock sounded at the front door.

His senses immediately went on high alert. He willed it to be Shelby, hoping she'd had a change of heart in the past hour and regretted her defiant dismissal of him. Though he fully intended to see her today, no matter how busy she claimed to be, it would be extremely gratifying if she were to take the first step for once. It would mean that they wouldn't have to start all over again, with those advance-retreat moves and countermoves, to regain lost ground.

And though he wasn't sure why, he knew that she'd strategically withdrawn from him. From the way she'd run from the car into her parents' house, it was clear that she was determined to put the friendly intimacy of last night firmly behind her.

And he was not going to let her do it. Garrett's blue eyes glinted with the fiery McGrath determination. He and Shelby would pick up the threads of friendly intimacy and take it further, to the all-encompassing intimacy that could exist between a man and a woman. The prospect stirred his blood and he strode to the door, hard and hungry with expectation.

Laney Halford stood on the small porch, wearing a very brief, purple, gold and green bikini, a pair of high-heeled sandals, and an alluring seductive smile. All that was missing was the tiara on her head and the sash reading Miss Wherever, he thought sardonically. The hot surging of his body instantly ceased, as if he'd been doused with a bucket of ice water.

"Room service," Laney announced throatily, holding up a small round tray containing two tall frothy drinks. "I thought you could use something special after your ordeal last night."

"You've seen Shelby?" That interested him, far more than Laney in full seduction mode.

"Yes, poor thing." Laney laughed prettily. "She looked like she'd just crawled out of a swamp. I believe she felt that way, too. She ranted on and on about what a miserable time she'd had last night. I felt sorry for her, of course, but after listening to her carry on, I found myself feeling sorrier for you. I know what a wretched disposition Shelby has, and I'm sure she didn't suffer in silence in that dumpy motel. You must have had a terrible night."

Garrett watched her, his blue eyes assessing. "So you've come to offer solace and succor?"

Laney dimpled. "I've come to present you with your very own Halford House Goddess."

"Are you by any chance referring to yourself?" he asked incredulously.

Laney chose to take his arch remark as a compliment. She tilted one hip and the motion caused her full breasts to jut forward. "A Halford House Goddess is a drink, silly." She giggled girlishly. "It's an original specialty of the house. One of the bartenders invented it a few years ago and named it in my honor. It goes down very smoothly, Garrett. I know you'll enjoy it." Her tone and her eyes implied that there was a lot more he could enjoy that afternoon, if he were willing.

Garrett eyed the white ice-creamy drink. His gaze flicked to Laney's petite but voluptuous figure, so lushly displayed in the bikini. The high thin heels added a blatantly alluring touch. This woman left no doubts that she was available for the asking.

But he wasn't asking. "I appreciate your concern," he said dryly. "But I don't drink in the afternoon, particularly when I'm working." He nodded toward the desk with its telephone and facsimile machine that had been installed at his request yesterday, during his absence.

"I'm due to be linked into a conference call and then I have to—" He broke off. He wasn't going to explain himself any further. The bottom line was that he wasn't interested in sampling a Halford House Goddess or Laney Halford's obvious charms. Had Shelby arrived at his door, unwashed in yesterday's wrinkled shorts and shirt or starched and stiff in one of those prim business suits she favored, he would have dumped the conference call without pause.

"I guess what I'm saying is, thanks but no thanks, Laney."

Laney's eyes narrowed to slits and a flash of pure rage momentarily marred her lovely features. But she quickly rearranged them into a sweet expression of regret. "I understand how busy you must be, Garrett. After all, you're an important executive of a multimillion-dollar corporation. Unlike Shelby, I appreciate your success with Family Fun Inns. She might look down on you and your motels as low class, but I don't. That's one of the many differences between Shelby and me. I admire other people's accomplishments—she's only interested in her own."

Garrett gazed at her impassively. "I see."

And he did. Laney's tactics were as subtle as a terrorist's bombing. He tried to imagine his own sisters trying to undermine each other, the way Laney did Shelby. He found the concept unfathomable. The McGrath sisters all possessed formidable tempers, so quarrels were certainly not unheard of, but innate family loyalty would prevent any one of them from deliberate sibling sabotage à la Laney Halford.

"You're something, Laney," he said with a smile that didn't reach his icy blue eyes. "You're really something."

Accustomed to unabashed admiration from men dazed by her beauty, Laney completely misinterpreted his sarcasm and his cold smile, taking them as compliments due. "You're something, too, Garrett." Her tone sounded calculatedly husky, and she wiggled closer to him, her movements equally studied.

She would have brushed against him if Garrett hadn't retreated several steps. "Hey, watch that tray," he said testily. "You almost doused me with those drinks. And I want to wear a Halford House Goddess even less than I want to drink one."

Laney shot him a look cold enough to freeze fire. "You don't have to snap at me!" she snapped at him.

"Don't I? How else can I make you go away? You don't seem to respond to subtle hints."

Laney gasped with indignant outrage. She pivoted around, no small feat in such high skinny heels, and stalked off. She'd gone only a few steps when she turned again and hurled the tray at him. Her aim was off. The glasses struck the wall of the cottage and then hit the ground, smashing to smithereens and soaking the walk with the thick, gooey white liquid.

"Have a cleaning crew sent over, will you?" he called after her as she rushed away, the height of the heels forcing her to take inefficient, mincing steps. Garrett didn't stick around to watch.

He went back inside, closing the door firmly behind him.

Eight

Shelby entered Miss York's office with some trepidation. Her father's secretary was seated at her desk, deeply engrossed in her typing, the very picture of formidable efficiency.

Miss York glanced up at her, clearly not pleased by Shelby's impromptu appearance. But Shelby didn't take the secretary's dour grimace personally. Miss York did not approve of any unscheduled visitor. If the President of the United States himself decided to drop in unannounced on Arthur Halford, Miss York would greet him with the same frown of disapproval she was bestowing on Shelby.

"I was wondering if my father is in and if I can see him?" Shelby was at her most respectful. She understood Miss York's need for order and routine; she required them herself. For a bleak moment, Shelby wondered if she were looking at a version of herself in the future. An executive Miss York whose every hour was regimented with no room for spontaneity, whose whole life revolved around Halford House.

She forced herself to shake off her dark mood. She was here to work, and she was dressed for it, in her charcoal-pinstriped summer wool suit and crisp white blouse. Her hair was swept back in its tight, untouchable chignon. She felt competent and professional, eager to do the job. Work had always been her panacea, dating back to her school days when she'd labored industriously over homework assignments.

After exchanging a few words over the intercom, Miss York motioned for Shelby to enter her father's office. Arthur Halford was seated behind his desk, a wary expression on his face.

"I understand you spent the night with Garrett McGrath," he said without preamble.

Shelby tried vainly to stem the hot blush sweeping through her. "It wasn't exactly like that, Dad," she said quickly. Who'd told him? And what had he been told?

"Is that why you're here?" Halford pressed. "Did he say or do anything that...uh, upset you?"

Astonished, Shelby stared at her father. Was this his way of asking if Garrett McGrath had, well, not treated her with the proper respect? She was flabbergasted. She couldn't ever remember him exhibiting such paternal concern, not even when she'd been a teenager just starting to date. It occurred to her that despite his display of professional assistance, perhaps her father didn't quite trust Garrett due to his low-end origins. That seemed patently unfair.

"Garrett was a perfect gentleman, Dad," she reassured him firmly. "He and I..." She was blushing again and annoyed with herself for it. "We both made the best of an unpleasant situation," she finished briskly. "And I know it's late, but I'm here to work."

Halford looked at her hard for a long moment. "Very well, I have an assignment for you." He reached into the top drawer of his desk and pulled out a folder. "Take this to McGrath. And stay with him until he reads it."

Shelby's first instinct was to protest. She didn't want to see Garrett, not now. After all, she'd spent the last hour or so trying to shove him out of her mind while vowing to keep her distance, thus thwarting his promise of an affair. She cleared her throat. "Couldn't Paul take it to him?"

"No, dammit, he can't!" snarled her father. "I don't understand you, Shelby. You come barging in here, demanding something to do and when I give you an assignment, you try to slough it off on Paul Whitley. Is that why you brought him here from California? To be your flunky?"

He fairly flung the folder at her. "Now take this to McGrath. I don't want any more complaints from you. And I don't want to see you for the rest of the day, either," he added, punching the buttons on his phone in an unmistakable gesture of dismissal.

Shelby took the folder and walked slowly from the office. She'd deserved that, she told herself bracingly. Her father's frustration with her was certainly understandable. She had barged in, demanded work, and then tried to reject the work he'd given her. As an executive, she wouldn't cotton to such insubordination, either. She glanced down at the folder. She would see to it that Garrett received it immediately.

As she walked through the lobby, she happened to catch a glimpse of herself in the big gilded mirror hanging above a Queen Anne chair newly upholstered in Halford green. Her attire was proper and appropriate for her position, of course, but all she could think of was Garrett's reaction to the similarly proper, appropriate attire that she'd worn to Key West. She imagined him opening the door of cottage 101 and making some wisecrack about her suit and the inadvisability of wearing any kind of wool when the heat and humidity had everyone else in cotton shorts and shirts.

He probably wouldn't stop with remarks about her suit, either. He would undoubtedly view her starched, tailored blouse, her dark-tinted stockings and her sensible pumps as additional fodder for his jokes. And she was certain he would be unable to resist making some comment about her hair. Though she'd chosen an ideal style for the seriously career-oriented woman that she was, perhaps she ought to modify it somewhat before she saw Garrett again. Maybe she should let her hair down, loose and casual, so he couldn't make any more pointed cracks about her too-tight chignon. Why give him a reason to divert his attention from the work she was bringing him?

Shelby nodded her head decisively. Since her presence at his cottage was strictly work related, it would be a mistake to distract him from it. And since her precision work-related wardrobe and hairstyle seemed to provide him with such amusement, it would be a wise move on her part to remove that source of frivolity.

Shelby stopped at her parents' house before making her delivery to Garrett. In record time, she shed her business suit for a floral-print sundress that tied at the neck, the long, gauzy skirt billowing around her calves. She also slipped on a pair of pastel espadrilles and brushed her hair so that it curved, soft and shiny, around her shoulders.

Now no one could fault her attire, climate-wise, she assured herself, glancing with satisfaction in her bedroom mirror. Her appearance, though it did not meet her own standards of professional formality, nevertheless would not provide Garrett with an excuse to focus jovially on her rather than the important business at hand.

Feeling validated as a businesswoman—she would always put Halford House first, even at the expense of her own professional image—Shelby set out for cottage 101 and Garrett McGrath.

She was about to knock on the door when it was flung open. Fortunately, her reflexes were quick and she jumped aside before Garrett, who was striding through the doorway, slammed directly into her.

He halted in his tracks and the two stood in silence, staring at each other.

"I didn't know you were out here," he said at last. "I didn't see you, I almost knocked you over." He paused, his blue eyes assessing her from head to toe. "Are you all right?"

"Oh, sure, I'm fine." She laughed nervously. "I'm fast on my feet. Good thing, too. I can't tell you how many run-away luggage carts I've had to dodge over the years or the—" Shelby broke off, embarrassed. She was babbling like a gauche and giddy adolescent. The realization sobered her, enabling her to swiftly compose herself. "I've come at a bad time. Obviously, you were going out."

He was wearing a pair of Halford green swim trunks with the Halford crest imprint. She knew he had to have purchased the suit at the Sun 'n' Swim shop in the hotel arcade. "You should've sprung for the matching camp shirt, too," she advised, raking her eyes over the T-shirt he wore, which boldly proclaimed Key Limes From Key West. The shirt also sported a decal: key limes with arms and legs, wearing hats and sunglasses and dancing in a conga line, a blatant rip-off of the California raisin commercials.

"That T-shirt you have on is even more hideous than your Florida oranges one, and that is no small feat," Shelby observed trenchantly.

"You don't like my souvenir shirt?" Garrett glanced down at his shirt rather proudly. "I bought it yesterday while you were browsing in that gallery with all the tasteful pottery and posters."

"Yes, I recall that you lasted about three minutes in that gallery before heading off to find one of your ubiquitous T-shirt shops."

"And I recall that you stayed in that gallery for what felt like an eternity. I finally had to drag you out."

"I was in there less than twenty minutes. Unfortunately, tasteful doesn't hold your interest for very long."

"Well, I'm willing to be educated. I'm always open to something new." He smiled, a slow and sexy smile that made his dark blue eyes crinkle. "Are you?"

Before she could move away, he cupped her bare shoulders with his hands, kneading the delicate bones with his fingers. Shelby knew she should get herself out of his reach. She tried to take a step away but he didn't relinquish his hold on her. Instead he began to caress her arms, stroking the

length of them, sweeping slowly up and down, his fingertips feathering her skin.

"Garrett, I don't... You can't... This isn't..." She took
a deep breath and started over. "You're busy, you were
planning to go swimming," she observed, her voice oddly
high and thready.

"I was coming to get you," he corrected. "I thought we'd
go to the beach for a while. But I'd much rather stay here
with you," he added huskily.

Shelby was acutely aware of his eyes on her, as they
flicked lazily but intently over her body. She felt his gaze as
an almost tangible touch, every part of her tightening and
tingling in response. He wanted her, she knew it. His face
silently but unmistakably bespoke desire.

She felt as if she were melting under the heated intensity
of his gaze. Vaguely she remembered the folder from her
father, the reason why she was here. But as she stood mesmerized by Garrett's deep blue eyes, her body flushing with
need and desire, the reason why she'd come seemed increasingly irrelevant. The folder slipped from her fingers
and fell to the ground, unnoticed by either of them.

"It's going to be good between us, Shelby." Garrett's
voice dropped, becoming lower and thicker. "I promise,
sweetheart."

His mouth covered hers, insistent and rapacious, taking
full possession of her lips without any preliminaries. He
pressed her tightly against him, one hand holding her head,
the other arching her into the hard masculine cradle of his
thighs.

Wildly, helplessly, Shelby felt herself catch fire. A tempestuous wave of emotion swept through her and she held
him closer, responding to his kiss with a fierce hunger all her
own. The force of his male arousal throbbed insistently
against her and she felt an unexpected tenderness for him.
She wanted to assuage this desire of his and satisfy her own
voluptuous yearnings. Never before had she experienced
these urgent and enthralling needs. They seemed to come
together in a passionate fire storm, sending her spinning out

of control and into a wild world where order and routine were irrelevant, where emotion and sensation reigned supreme.

She was so lost in the fiery wonder of their passion that she was caught unaware when he suddenly lifted his mouth from hers to scoop her up into his arms. She gave a small gasp of surprise and automatically clasped her arms around his neck, hanging on for dear life. The sensation of being lifted and carried, of not having her feet firmly on solid ground, was disorienting. And being disoriented was not a pleasant sensation for one who prized being in control of herself and the situation at all times.

"Put me down!" she ordered tightly. Her passion-induced mindlessness had abruptly dissolved, replaced by her usual self-protective hypervigilance. She tensed, bracing herself for a fall.

Garrett merely grinned and carried her inside, pausing only to kick the front door shut.

The sensation of moving through the air with no control over the motion was becoming increasingly alarming. "Garrett, I'm not kidding," she warned. She tried to kick her feet in protest but succeeded only in losing one shoe.

"Honey, neither am I."

Her nails dug into his shoulders. He had hastened his stride and she made the mistake of looking up. The rampant sexuality in his blue eyes unnerved her as much as the fleeting glimpses of the ceiling passing overhead. She went limp and still and swiftly lowered her eyes to the ground.

Seconds later, he dropped her onto the bed. She landed with a bounce, then quickly scrambled to the other side, losing her other shoe in the process. She was incensed. "For your information, Garrett McGrath, I do not like being carried."

"Yeah, I noticed that."

"And I also don't like being bounced on the bed like a...a rubber ball."

"I thought you'd want to check out the quality of the mattress." Garrett pulled his T-shirt over his head. "It sure beats that lumpy piece of junk at the Seagull last night, hmm?'' He tossed his shirt over the nearby settee.

Shelby stood on the other side of the bed, trembling with nerves and temper and pent-up desire. Her hazel eyes were fastened compulsively on him, taking in every detail of his strong, corded arms and muscular chest. Her gaze traced the mat of dark, wiry hair to the indentation of his navel where it arrowed lower, beneath the waistband of his swim trunks. She swallowed, hard.

Garrett was smoothing his hand over the surface of the bed. ''There isn't a single spring in this mattress to stick out and jab you. I counted at least seven at the Seagull.''

''I know what you're trying to do, Garrett,'' Shelby said sternly, backing away toward the window.

''I should expect so,'' Garrett agreed. He held out his hand to her.

She shook her head and put her hands behind her back. ''You're trying to distract me by talking about the mattress and the Seagull Motel and—''

''I'm trying to recoup lost ground,'' Garrett admitted frankly, his blue eyes gleaming. ''I realize that I blundered big time by picking you up and carrying you in here.''

''Yes, you did. I hated it. I was positive you would drop me and I'd hit my head on the ground. I kept wondering how a cat manages to land on its feet after a fall and how I could do it, too.''

''Whew! I really did blow it.'' Garrett laughed and walked around the bed toward her. ''I was hoping to set a romantic mood and all you were thinking about were cats and aerodynamics and injuries.''

He had her cornered between the bed and the wall and the window. There was no way for her to avoid him unless she jumped onto the bed and bolted across it. Shelby considered doing just that as he approached her.

''Come here, baby,'' he said quietly, holding open his arms to her.

Shelby's eyes darted from him to the expanse of the king-size bed to the bedroom door that, though just across the room, seemed inaccessible and miles away. "I...can't do this, Garrett."

"Yes, you can." He was directly in front of her now and she stood stock-still as he untied the strings of her sundress at the nape of her neck. "You want me and you have to know how much I want you."

She shivered as he lowered the bodice of her dress. Before she had time to inhale, he'd unhooked her strapless white bra and bared her breasts. She stood before him, trembling with an edgy mixture of excitement and embarrassment, her breasts exposed to him.

"You're so beautiful," he murmured as he stared down at the milky white fullness of her pink-tipped breasts.

Even as she reeled in a sensual daze, Shelby couldn't let that pass. Laney was the beautiful one, not her. She shook her head, feeling compelled to set the record straight. "I'm not beautiful, I—"

"Yes, you are." His voice was soft and deep and hypnotically soothing. "You're beautiful and smart and funny and sexy as hell. You're also forthright and tough and those are two requirements when dealing with me."

"You don't cotton to sensitive, shrinking violets?" She hardly recognized the low, throaty voice as her own.

"Nope. Or devious little schemers," he added, thinking of Laney's appearance with the Halford Goddesses. "You're neither, thank God. You're perfect for me."

"You're deluded," she said, her face flushing. "I'm not perfect, Garrett."

"I didn't say you were. I said you were perfect *for me* and that's something else entirely. I wanted you from the first moment I laid eyes on you and the time we've spent together has only intensified that desire." His hands cupped her breasts with surprising gentleness. "You do know that, don't you, Shelby? That I want you very, very much."

She closed her eyes, leaning into him. She couldn't help herself. His big, warm hands felt so good on her breasts. There was a sharp sensual ache throbbing in her belly and a provocative heat raged between her legs, emboldening her.

"How much is that?" she whispered. "How much is very, very much?"

"More than anything I've ever wanted in my life," he said hoarsely. His deft fingers kneaded the rounded softness, then stroked her nipples, watching the buds tighten and darken under his caresses.

Shelby drew in a quick breath as sharp spirals of desire uncoiled deep within her. She felt lost in a thick, sweet fog that was blanketing her mind, as potent and intoxicating as last night's bottle of Circe's Spiced Rum. But today there was no alcohol involved, only emotion and sensation, heightened to degrees she'd never imagined.

Garrett's hands slid to her waist and pushed her dress over her hips where it fell to the floor and pooled around her ankles. She was left wearing only her white panties, a cotton bikini-style cut high on the leg and low around the hips. Such a small scrap of material didn't afford much protection from the intensity and urgency glittering in his blue eyes.

A shudder of desire shook her, but it was mixed with a nervous pang of apprehension.

He noticed and swiftly pulled her into his arms. "Don't be afraid of me, Shelby."

Her cheeks brushed the wiry-soft hair on his chest; she felt the hard warmth of his arms enfolding her. His palms smoothed over the length of her bare back, molding her closer, settling her firmly against him. Between her legs, she felt the thick, virile strength of him pressing insistently. The thin cloth of her panties and slick material of his swimsuit were the only barriers to the most intimate contact of all. The notion was both scary and exciting.

"I...don't know how good I'm going to be at this," Shelby murmured.

"Relax, sweetheart." He eased her gently down onto the bed and lay beside her, taking her hand in his. "There aren't going to be any performance reviews." He lifted her hand to his mouth, caressing it with his lips. "It isn't a matter of being good or bad at anything."

"I've always tried to be good at whatever I do." She turned her head and gazed at him, her hazel eyes earnest. "I have to admit that I don't have a lot of experience in this area, Garrett."

Garrett's lips quirked. "Try to keep in mind that this isn't a business interview, Shelby. A résumé or a list of references is not required."

"That's good, because I couldn't supply one."

She wondered if he'd heard her because he made no reply. He was touching her breasts, filling his palms with the high rounded softness, tracing the size and shape of her tautly beaded nipples with his fingertips. His hands moved leisurely yet thoroughly, drifting downward over the sleek slope of her stomach. When he slipped his fingers beneath the waistband of her panties, she sucked in her breath.

"Garrett, what I'm trying to say is that..." Her voice quivered as his hands tangled in the dark curls of her womanhood. Instinctively she pressed her thighs together.

"I know, baby. I know." With calm and firm assurance, he slipped his hand between her legs, applying an exquisite pressure that made her moan with pleasure. "I'm the first." His eyes gleamed with primal satisfaction as he gazed at her. He didn't know that it would mean so much to him, being Shelby's first lover. A streak of possessiveness he never knew he had surged through him. He vowed then and there that he would be her only lover, as well.

Shelby was mortified by her admission. She was nothing but a cliché, she railed to herself. She was the archetypal, nervous, overaged, old-fashioned fool! Why hadn't she just kept her mouth shut? He'd have found out the truth soon enough. What must he think of her? Probably that she was an archetypal, nervous, overaged, old-fashioned fool, that's what.

Her confidence plummeted, along with her ardor. The tantalizing, teasing intimacy of his fingers was too much. She grabbed his hand and lifted it away from her. He allowed her to do so, but held on to her hand, twining his fingers with hers.

"Go ahead and laugh," Shelby rasped, looking away. His stare was too penetrating and she had nowhere to hide. She felt vulnerable and uncertain and scorned herself for it. "I know I'm a misfit out of time and place. I always have been."

"What you are and always will be, is mine," Garrett countered.

It was definitely time to stop talking. She needed actions, not words to dispel her anxiety. He studied her profile as she lay, rigid and tense, beside him. Shelby Halford, a bona fide spitfire, was still a virgin. Who would've thought it? Yet the knowledge didn't come as a complete shock. She was so defensive and uptight, determined never to cede control, command or composure. Surrender would not come easily or naturally to her.

But her swift, hot arousal in response to his kisses and caresses proved to him that she was no ice maiden, that the passion in her was as fierce as her temper. She needed to feel secure enough to set it free. She needed a man who was both sexually aggressive and very reassuring. And he was that man.

"I'm going to make love to you, Shelby."

A shiver of desire raced through her as Garrett leaned over her. She gazed into his eyes, which were dark with passion and desire. Her pulses were pounding. He was going to make love to her and she wanted him to, so much. She hadn't realized just how much until this moment.

Her eyelids dropped shut at the touch of his mouth and she was instantly transported into a private world of pure sensation. His lips feathered hers, the tip of his tongue toyed with her mouth, seeking entrance. She instantly obliged him, and his tongue entered her mouth, probing and rubbing seductively against hers.

Shelby clung to him as they kissed and kissed, each kiss becoming deeper and hotter and more intimate, each melding into another in passionate fusion. Heated waves of sexual excitement washed over her and a slow, languorous warmth suffused her entire body. She wanted to be closer to him, much closer.

She wrapped herself around him, moving her body sinuously against his. When his hands cupped the taut, swollen fullness of her breasts, she whimpered his name. Her nipples were so sensitized they were almost painfully hard, but it was an exciting kind of pleasure-pain, a dizzying sensual dichotomy.

"You want me," Garrett murmured in husky satisfaction. "As much as I want you. Tell me, Shelby. I want to hear the words."

And she wanted to give them to him. "I want you, Garrett," she whispered dreamily. She felt as if she really were dreaming, the most erotic, romantic dream of her life. But it was real, he was real. And these primitive elemental feelings he evoked in her were not the ephemeral stuff of dreams nor simply the heat of sexual attraction.

She was in love with him. The flash of insight was shattering, jolting her out of her sensual daze. She stared at him for a stunned second. Being in love was twice as unnerving as the prospect of making love. If only he loved her, too....

"It's all right, sweetheart." Garrett's voice, sexy and low and reassuring, was at her ears. His lips moved slowly, sensuously, along the slender curve of her neck. "I know this is new to you but we're here together and you have nothing to fear."

Nothing to fear. His words reverberated in her head. How about being in love with a man who didn't love her? That was certainly a prospect designed to scare any discerning woman. And she couldn't delude herself into thinking that Garrett loved her. She knew he didn't. He talked about wanting her and she had no doubts that he did, but that was sex, something quite apart from love.

But then his mouth was on her breast, his tongue tracing concentric circles around her nipple until it stood out, tight and hard. A hungry little cry escaped from deep in her throat. The way he was making her feel rendered coherent thought impossible. And the appeal of coherent thought paled in comparison to the enthralling pleasure spinning through her. She'd always thought too much; thinking was both her offense and defense. But she didn't want to offend Garrett or to defend herself against him. Not now. All she wanted to do right now was to savor every lush sensation, to not think at all but simply *feel*.

Garrett's hand slipped lower and pulled off her panties in one deft sweep. She felt his fingers flex in the downy apex of her thighs, seeking and finding, and she gasped at his bold foray. Liquid fire burned through her veins. Her head tossed from side to side as he gently, lightly, probed her soft cleft, caressing her sensitive flesh with a sensual expertise that made her moan.

She was moist and swollen and her body quivered, drawing tight as a bowstring, as she surged upward against his hand. He was touching her, stroking her, his clever fingers inside her, driving her wild and making her part her legs wider in aching need.

He continued the sensual torment as she arched into him, clinging to him in urgent abandon. "Garrett, please!" she cried, not quite sure what she was pleading for. She shuddered as pleasure streaked through her, sharp and fast, radiating from her hot, damp center to every nerve and muscle in her body.

Crushed against him, she could feel the powerful strength of his arousal and she was filled with heady feminine pride. It was incredibly empowering to know that she could rouse this urgent need in him, that she could stoke the fire of desire within him.

She tugged at his swim trunks, her hands trembling, her eyes glittering with a passion that matched his own. It felt so right to give herself to him. He was the man she loved and she'd waited a lifetime for him. A hot flood of anticipation flowed through her. She wanted to see him, to feel him.....

Garrett helped her divest himself of his swimsuit and when her hands closed over him in eager anticipation, he groaned with pleasure. She fondled him, exploring his hard body, both fascinated and stirred by his virile male form.

"I want to be inside you," he growled, and the sexy rasp of his voice was as arousing as his caresses. His face tightened as he gazed down at her nude body, stretched invitingly before him. "We'll take it slow and easy—the first time." He flashed a smile of sensual promise that took her breath away.

"Yes," she whispered, reaching for him. "Yes, Garrett." He'd called it right when he had possessively claimed her as his own earlier. She was his, and she wanted to prove it with an aching, desperate urgency.

She surrendered completely to his unnerving, inexorable and totally thrilling penetration of her soft, slim body. For a few moments he lay still inside her as her body accommodated itself to his indomitable presence. He stroked her hair and kissed her, murmuring exciting words of praise and encouragement.

Slowly, her taut muscles relaxed and he began to move within her. Shelby reveled in the fullness of him deep inside her. It seemed perfectly natural for her to wrap her legs tightly around him, and the rhythmic motion of her hips came naturally, too. His thrusts were slow and careful at first, and then became harder, faster, as she matched him stroke for stroke in rapturous abandon.

Shelby gasped and cried out, writhing beneath him as a shimmering tension built and intensified. They moved together in frenzied passion, she arching wildly, he driving into her with an increasing power. His hands slid under her to grasp her bottom, lifting her higher and sending sudden, sharp bolts of pleasure exploding through her.

The sensual explosion rocked her, deep and strong, and her spasms of release drew Garrett into the mindless, swirling vortex of passion and pleasure that melted all boundaries between them, merging them and making them one.

"Shelby." Garrett's voice sounded softly in her ear.

She realized that she must have fallen asleep because the last thing she remembered was the heavy warm weight of him sprawled on top of her, their bodies still intimately joined, but now he lay beside her and she was curled spoon-fashion against him.

She smiled up at him as his mouth settled lazily over hers. Shelby responded at once, kissing him fiercely, posses-sively.

"I'm glad you dropped by to see me this afternoon." Lifting his mouth an inch or two above hers, Garrett's lips curved into a slow smile, his blue eyes lazy with sensual sat-isfaction. "After the way you flounced off earlier, I didn't think you would. I thought you'd fight your attraction for me every step of the way." His arms tightened around her. "But I was prepared to do whatever it took to keep you from winning that fight."

"Let's get one thing straight—I don't flounce," Shelby informed him huskily, stroking the strong, hard line of his jaw with gently caressive hands. "I might stalk regally away, but I've never flounced off in my life."

"Uh-huh." He clasped his hand around her nape, secur-ing her mouth for a lingering, deeply tender kiss.

Later, much later, they lay together, sated and replete in the warm afterglow of passion. And for the first time in a long while, Shelby recalled the initial reason why she'd come looking for Garrett. She toyed with the idea of letting him continue to believe that her arrival was a spontaneous de-cision, fueled by the potent chemistry between them. To drag in the prosaic world of business certainly deroman-ticized their encounter.

But she was too honest to lie, even by omission. "Gar-rett, I have sort of a confession to make," she began tenta-tively. "Remember when you said that you hadn't expected me to come here to see you today, that you thought I'd fight my attraction to you? Well, you were right."

"I was, hmm?" Garrett did not sound unduly con-cerned.

"I fully intended to stay away from you. In fact, I'd vowed to keep away from you," she said earnestly. "I wouldn't have come over here if my father hadn't insisted that I bring you a folder—" She sat up abruptly. "Good heavens, the folder! I didn't give it to you, did I? No, of course I didn't. But I can't remember what I did with it."

"Who cares?" Garrett tried to pull her back down to him.

"Garrett, this is important. My father told me to stay with you until you'd read the contents of that folder. We have to find it." She jumped out of bed, then realized that she was naked. She met his wry, interested gaze and blushed.

Garrett took pity on her and climbed out of bed to hand her the official Halford House white terry bathrobe. While she wrapped herself in it, he pulled on his swim trunks and headed out of the bedroom to the front door.

He found the folder where she'd dropped it, in front of the cottage. His eyes drifted to the congealing remains of the Halford House Goddesses surrounded by the shattered glasses. Laney obviously hadn't called for a cleaning crew. She took direction about as well as she took rejection, he thought dryly. Which was not well at all.

Back inside, Shelby slipped her arms around his waist from behind and snuggled against him. "I hope your ego isn't too bruised from hearing that it was my father's orders and not your irresistible appeal that brought me over here today." Her hands slipped provocatively inside the waistband of his swim trunks.

"Yeah, but it was your overwhelming attraction to me that made you take off your dress-for-success suit of armor and your orthopedic panty hose before you came over. When you showed up in that sexy little dress with your legs bare, I knew that—"

"I can see that your ego is fully intact. No worries along that score." She traced the whorl of his navel with her thumb. "Aren't you going to read what's in the folder?"

"Believe me, baby, I couldn't care less. Let's just forget about the stupid folder and go back to bed." He turned, reaching for her, but she artfully eluded his grasp.

"Business before pleasure. Work before play," Shelby teased. Grinning, she snatched the folder from his hands and opened it. There were several color brochures describing Halford House and listing the reasons why the discerning vacationer would choose to stay there.

"This is it?" She stared at them in confusion. "But they're just promotional material. Why would Dad insist that I bring these over to you immediately and stay until you'd read them?"

"Honey, I have no idea why your father does the things he does. The man is an enigma to me."

"Unless..." Shelby stared at Garrett, her hazel eyes wide with wonder. "Do you suppose Dad was matchmaking? That he wanted us to get together and deliberately sent me over here to you, knowing—or at least hoping—that when we saw each other we would—"

"Art Halford as cupid," Garrett cut in. "What a concept."

"What a concept," Shelby echoed softly. Had her father noticed the attraction between her and Garrett and decided to give her fledgling romance a helping hand? It was a most un-Arthur-Halfordlike thing to do. She couldn't remember her father ever being interested in her personal life, certainly he'd never involved himself in it.

She thought of his outburst when she had initially refused to bring the folder to Garrett. No wonder he had exploded. He had been trying to help her and had become understandably frustrated when she'd tried to thwart him.

Shelby looked at Garrett, her eyes glowing with warmth and love. Thanks to Arthur Halford's well-intentioned scheme, she was with the man she loved instead of sitting home alone, trying to fight her own feelings. Vaguely, she recalled that those feelings were based on something very real—the fear that Garrett McGrath intended to have a short-term affair with her before heading on his merry way.

But those fears didn't seem as threatening now. Not after what she and Garrett had shared. Shelby draped her arms around his neck and went up on tiptoe to nuzzle his neck. A burst of joyous feminine confidence flowed through her at his instant response.

It wasn't going to be so easy for him to walk away from her. She would see to that.

Nine

Shelby and Garrett were together constantly, spending nearly every waking moment with each other—and their nonwaking moments, too. It was remarkably easy to tell her parents that she'd decided to take a broom-closet-size room in the hotel, to be in the center of the action, rather than stay at home. They asked no questions, making it clear that where she spent her nights was of no concern to them.

And Shelby chose to spend her nights in cottage 101 with Garrett, making love into the late hours then falling asleep, her body tucked into his, his strong arms wrapped possessively around her.

Garrett made a few day trips to Buffalo for business reasons, always returning in the evening to a passionate reunion with Shelby. And then, one afternoon he called from New York to tell her that an emergency had arisen, requiring him to spend the night in the city.

She well understood business emergencies, of course, but her body couldn't seem to adjust to the sudden lack of Garrett's attentions, of the sensual satisfaction she'd come to crave. She lay in the bed they'd shared, tossing and turning restlessly, tensions building within her. Even after she'd finally managed to fall asleep, she missed the presence of his warm, solid body beside her.

The emergency extended to another day, and Shelby decided to make use of the broom-closet-like room in the hotel that night. She might sleep better there, a place where there were no memories of him, of the two of them together.

But it seemed she was doomed to another fitful night. A change of location did nothing to ease the ache of Garrett's absence.

She awoke at dawn to hear an odd, rattling sound. By the time her foggy brain discerned that it was the sound of the old-fashioned lock on the door being turned, the door was opened. Garrett stood on the threshold.

Shelby blinked, wondering if she was dreaming. "Garrett?" she mumbled drowsily.

"None other, sweetheart." His voice was a husky rasp that sent sensuous shivers tingling along her spine. He crossed the room in brisk strides, pulling off his jacket, his shirt, his tie.

Shelby was wide-awake now, alert and on fire with need. She knelt up on the bed and reached for him.

His mouth was on hers, his hands grasping her body. Shelby responded with an ardent hunger of her own. She hadn't known it was possible to miss someone so desperately. But length of time had nothing to do with it. Her need for him existed in a place where there were no such concepts as space and time.

Garrett kissed her mouth, her neck, then slid the elasticized peasant-style neckline of her floral-print nightgown over her shoulders to kiss their white softness. Shelby clung to him, moaning.

One of his big hands was inside her nightgown, cupping her breast, the other delved beneath the hem, between her legs.

They lay down on the bed together, tugging at their remaining clothes, tossing them aside. Their kisses were deep and fierce, their caresses intimate and urgent. They'd spent many hours learning to please each other, and their erotic expertise stoked the fires burning hotly within them.

"You're ready for me, precious?" Garrett murmured deeply. It was both a question and a command.

Shelby gave him a sultry, sexy smile. "I was ready for you the moment I saw you standing in the door."

"I was ready for you before I even got to the door," Garrett countered, enjoying their small game of one-up-manship. "That's why I made the staff work till nearly midnight to tie up the loose ends and then hopped a plane down here. I couldn't be away from you for another night."

Shelby thought it the most romantic declaration she'd ever heard. "Oh, Garrett, I hated being away from you, too," she confessed on a sigh.

"I'm here now," he said, his eyes glittering with a passion that thrilled her.

She opened herself to him, and he surged inside her. She was hot creamy softness, tightly sheathing him, and they both groaned with pleasure.

They moved together in a primal, sensual rhythm, and the shimmering tension built and grew and exploded into a fire storm of rapture. The sweet flames engulfed them, sweeping them both to a simultaneous, tumultuous climax.

There was time for a tender, lingering kiss before both fell into a deep and satisfied sleep.

Garrett had promised to shake up Shelby's usual routine, and he did. He was innately curious about his surroundings and the two of them took a number of excursions to various attractions in the south Florida area.

They saw everything from the wealthy glamour of Palm Beach to the alligators in the swamps of the Everglades National Park. Garrett inevitably dragged her into his beloved tourist traps—not even Palm Beach was immune to cheap souvenirs!—to purchase junk that she simply had to ridicule. But it was done with humor and affection. Even their sparring these days was all in good fun.

They made unscheduled visits to those Family Fun Inns that were within a day's driving distance, where the full-occupancy rate at each motel continued to astound Shelby. She remembered to ask whether the rooms with green doors were always the last to be rented, wowing the local managers with her insider's knowledge, and bringing a private smile to Garrett's lips. She began to feel a proprietary pride in the company as they checked out the renowned playgrounds and made sure that the "three C's of Family Fun"—cleanliness, courtesy, and cheap room rates—were being upheld.

When they weren't traveling for business or pleasure, they discharged their excess energy by running or swimming together in the pool or in the ocean. They played tennis and rented boats to sail. They danced and they made love, sometimes hot and hard and fast, sometimes with languid, lingering leisure.

Shelby hardly noticed how little time she was spending on Halford House concerns. Garrett was busy for periods each day conducting Family Fun Inn business but, as her father had yet to give her any job-related responsibilities, Shelby's career was temporarily on hold.

As was Paul Whitley's. Though Paul had been assigned a few minor tasks, he had no actual title or job description, either. He was seen constantly in Laney's company, and Shelby sometimes wondered where their romance would lead. Had her sister finally fallen in love? There had always been men in love with Laney, although it had never been reciprocal on her part.

But Shelby was too happy to worry about anything these days, not Halford House or her career, not Paul or Laney or the prospect of displeasing her father. Not even the threat of Garrett's eventual departure disturbed her because it had ceased to be a threat. She felt confident, she felt secure and sensual and free. Her life was engrossing and satisfying, with no time for edginess, anxiety or recriminations.

* * *

One sunny October afternoon, Shelby swung idly on the wooden glider in the gazebo, surrounded by lush tropical flowers and greenery, conjuring up memories of the previous night's passionate scene with Garrett. The visual images evoked tactile sensations and she felt her body grow warm and flushed and aroused. She wanted him. The desire was a pang so strong, she had to catch her breath.

How long until she saw him again? Shelby glanced at her watch. He'd told her he had some business to conduct and they had parted after lunch: Garrett to his cottage and the vital phone and facsimile connections to his company and she to wander through the gardens. She hadn't even bothered to ask her father if there were any hotel-related projects for her to do, for she knew he would fob her off with an "ask Garrett what he wants you to do."

The lack of structure and unprecedented amount of free time would have previously driven her into a maelstrom of impatience and anxiety. Not now. She could wile away hours reminiscing about her times with Garrett, contemplating what he said and did, what he looked like while he was saying and doing it. And there was always the delicious anticipation of their next encounter to further fuel her daydreams.

When she saw Laney and Paul approach her, she tensed. Laney would undoubtedly want to indulge in some of her verbal target practice but Shelby was not in a contentious mood. Far from it. She was feeling content and benevolent toward the world, and that included her sister. And she was thoroughly enjoying her sweet reverie. If she couldn't be alone with Garrett, she wanted to be alone with her thoughts of him. Making conversation with anybody was an unwelcome distraction.

"Shelby, have you heard the news?" Laney burst out. Her dark eyes were slitted and stormy, her mouth twisted into a scowl. Still, she looked beautiful enough to cause heads to turn and jaws to gape.

Shelby remembered the times when the sight of her sister's incomparable beauty had filled her with a great sense of her own inadequacies. She smiled softly. Not anymore. Garrett's attention and admiration had given her a confidence in herself that she'd never possessed before.

"What news is that, Laney?" she asked.

"The news that is going to wipe that silly smile right off your face," Laney snapped. The vindictive edge in her voice indicated that she'd enjoy seeing it happen.

Shelby sighed. "What's wrong, Laney?" Her dreamy smile was already gone.

"Shelby, you must try to stay calm," Paul said, pausing to inhale deeply. He seemed to be bracing himself. "We saw Oliver Tate with your father. You've probably heard of Tate. He owns the Wild Waters Resort in Idaho and two other exclusive resorts in the Southwest."

"I know who Oliver Tate is," Shelby said impatiently. Who in the industry didn't know of the wealthy hotelier? "What about him?"

"Daddy has sold Halford House to him!" Laney announced, her voice rising.

For a moment, Shelby didn't react at all. Though she'd heard the words, she couldn't seem to assimilate them. She rose slowly to her feet, her stomach lurching queerly, as if she'd been kicked in the gut. "Laney, that can't be true. You must've misinterpreted what—"

"I didn't misinterpret anything," Laney countered bitterly. "I asked Mr. Tate straight-out if he'd bought Halford House and that wicked old coot just laughed and said yes." She broke a flower from its stem, viciously ripping away the petals and scattering them to the ground.

"I've been hearing rumors for the past week or so that Halford House has been sold, only the buyer remained a secret." Paul's voice matched his somber expression. "When Oliver Tate showed up and headed straight for your father's office, I put one and one together. Then Laney confronted him about it and—"

"Rumors? What rumors?" Shelby cried bewilderedly. "I haven't heard a single rumor. I—"

"That's because you've been spending all your time chasing after Garrett McGrath," Laney said acidly. "The rumors have been running rampant. I'm sure your dear Mr. McGrath heard them himself."

"Garrett never mentioned any rumors," Shelby whispered. *Halford House sold?* No, it couldn't be true, her mind cried out in denial. Halford House was home, her past, present and future all bound up into one. She'd had to leave it to study and to work, to become worthy of it. And when she'd returned she had envisioned staying forever.

And now Laney and Paul were telling her that forever was right now. "If . . . if Garrett knew—" she began.

"Of course, he knew. If he didn't tell you, it's probably because he knew it would distract you and he didn't want anything to interfere with his campaign to get you in to bed." Laney tossed her head and her thick, dark hair cascaded dramatically around her shoulders. "His very successful campaign, I might add. Everybody knows about your affair with Garrett McGrath, Shelby. You've hardly been discreet, the way you're always hanging on him and mooning over him like a love-struck adolescent." Laney's tone was particularly venomous. She had obviously taken Garrett's preference for Shelby as a personal insult.

"Shelby, the sale of Halford House makes my position here extremely uncertain, to say the least," Paul said worriedly. "Even though your father made no commitments to me, I assumed that when you took over—" He broke off and continued on a more accusatory note. "I gave up a promising career at Casa del Marina to come here based on your word that there would be a job for me, an executive position in management, but with Oliver Tate as owner of Halford House, the situation changes completely."

"If it's true, everything changes for me, too, Paul," Shelby reminded him. She forced herself to keep her composure and her temper under control. Going emotionally ballistic would serve no useful purpose. "But I can't believe that Dad would sell the place without a single word to

any of us. No matter what rumors you heard or what Oliver
Tate said—''

"Why, here's Garrett now," Laney cried shrilly. "We can
ask him exactly what he does or doesn't know."

All heads turned to see Garrett approaching the gazebo,
his stride brisk and purposeful as always. Shelby's heart
skipped a beat at the sight of him and she felt an odd relief
trickle through her. Just seeing him made her spirits soar
and infused her with optimism.

Impulsively, she rushed to meet him. She definitely was
not being discreet, Shelby thought wryly. Laney had called
that one right.

However, Garrett seemed delighted with her lack of
proper restraint. "I've been tracking you down for the past
half hour," he said warmly, snatching both her hands and
drawing her to him. "Finally, someone remembered seeing
you head out here."

Shelby lifted her face and gazed into his deep blue eyes.
It would've been natural for them to kiss hello, but the
presence of Laney and Paul, plus the shocking news bulle-
tin restrained her. "We, uh, have company," she murmured, inclining her head toward the gazebo where Laney
and Paul stood, glaring.

Garrett was not pleased to see them, either. "I'll tell them
that we're due somewhere right now and we can make a fast
getaway."

"We need to talk to them, Garrett," Shelby said urgently. "They've heard this rumor..."

Her voice trailed off and she swallowed hard around the
lump that suddenly blocked her throat. Let Laney tell him,
she couldn't. A rush of tears filled her eyes and she quickly
blinked them away.

Garrett gazed down at her in concern. "Sweetheart,
what's the matter?"

She didn't have a chance to reply. Laney and Paul bore
down on them with the force of a runaway train.

"Garrett, did you know that Daddy sold Halford House to Oliver Tate?" Laney demanded, her dark eyes glowing with malicious rage.

Garrett stood still, looking from Shelby to Laney to Paul. He took it all in—Shelby's pain and confusion, Laney's vengeful fury, Paul's worried self-concern. He'd been in tight situations before, where negotiations hinged on maintaining the correct expression and producing the right words, and normally he thrived on the challenge and its accompanying adrenaline rush. But not this time. The stakes were way too high and far too personal. He could lose Shelby forever if he mishandled the crisis.

Garrett immediately rejected that possibility. His eyes narrowed with a determination known to anyone who'd ever dealt with him on an adversarial basis. He'd garnered a reputation for ruthlessness when it came to getting what he wanted professionally and he saw no reason not to extend that talent to his personal life as well. He would do whatever it took to keep Shelby.

Laney interpreted his silence and his expression in her own way. "You did know about the sale!" she cried, harsh and accusing.

"I wish you would have mentioned something about it to us," Paul muttered. He was irritated but trying not to show it, not to the alleged owner of the Blue Springs Resort.

Garrett cleared his throat. "I hadn't heard that Oliver Tate bought Halford House." Well, that was certainly true enough. He knew from long experience that it was best to stick to the truth—or at least the closest thing to it—when in a precarious position. "From what I've heard, Tate is a longtime friend of Art's. He happened to be in the south Florida area and decided to stay at Halford House for a couple days, mainly to golf with Art. He arrived last night. Is that when and how the rumors started?" he asked.

"They started because they're true, which makes them fact and not rumor," Laney replied angrily. "And I think you knew all about the sale, Garrett McGrath. You've certainly been buddy-buddy enough with Daddy to have been told about it." She stared from Garrett to Shelby, pinning her sister with a cold-eyed glare. "There's just something about your boyfriend that I don't trust, Shelby."

And that something is his judgment because he wanted me and not you, Shelby thought. Laney's vindictiveness was wearing on her; the fast getaway Garrett proposed beckoned irresistibly. She looked up at Garrett, squeezing his hand. "Did you come to remind me that we're due somewhere right now?"

"I most certainly did. Come on, we're already late." He started back down the path, pulling Shelby after him.

They broke into a partial run and didn't slow down until they were on the beach, near the isolated stretch where they'd first kissed. This time Garrett didn't suggest a fully clothed dip in the ocean.

He turned to Shelby, his blue eyes dark and serious. "Are you okay?" he asked with such genuine concern that her eyes filled with tears.

"They have to be wrong, Garrett. My father couldn't have sold Halford House to Oliver Tate."

"Come here, sweetheart."

He dropped to the sand, then reached for her hand and tugged it. She automatically sat down next to him, and he draped his arm around her shoulders, pulling her against him. She nestled there, her head in the hollow of his chest, savoring the hard, warm strength of him. One big hand stroked her hair gently and the other one reached for her hand and interlocked his fingers with hers.

They sat together, closely, quietly, holding hands and staring at the waves cresting and breaking, then receding out to sea. The scene was so peacefully hypnotic that it took a while for it to dawn on Shelby that Garrett's silence was an ominous sign. He had not dismissed outright Laney and Paul's assertion that Halford House had been sold, he'd merely said that he hadn't heard Oliver Tate was the buyer.

His quiet solicitude was yet another sign that something was not right. She had been with Garrett often enough to know that when they were alone together in a very private setting, he was not content to simply hold her, not unless they were both satiated and exhausted from spent passion. Which was certainly not the case here.

Something had to be troubling him or he would be kissing her, trying to slip his hands underneath the soft blue cotton of her summer sweater to unfasten her bra....

"It's true, isn't it? My father has sold Halford House." Her voice trembled.

"Yes, it's true," Garrett said solemnly.

Pain seared her. "Why? Why would he do it? This is more than just a resort hotel, it's our home. Three generations of Halfords have lived here and—"

"I'm not going to plead your father's case for him but there are a few things you might want to consider, Shelby. You were away for ten years. The nephew who was supposed to take over the place after the designated heir died turned out to be an irresponsible goof-off who couldn't be trusted to set his alarm clock, let alone run a business."

"But *I* could have been named the new designated heir," Shelby cried. "I was the logical choice to succeed Dad. I'd already established a career in hotel management and I've always looked on Halford House as my...my birthright." A tear trickled down her cheek. "My birthright. That sounds stupid and medieval, doesn't it?"

"No." He brushed the tear away with the pad of his thumb. "But maybe your father didn't realize how you felt about the place, Shelby. He's not what I'd call the sensitive, intuitive type. Did you come right out and ask him, 'Dad, may I take over Halford House when you retire?'"

Shelby shook her head. "I guess part of me was afraid he'd say no, that he wouldn't think I was competent enough. So I thought I'd show him that I was. Mom mentioned over the phone that Dad was thinking of retirement, though she didn't say it would be so soon. I thought he'd stay on several more years and I decided to come back to Halford House and work alongside my father, to prove to him that I was the one to take over when he retired.

"I was tired of the Casa del Marina and I was tired of California," Shelby said slowly. "I wanted to make some changes in my life, to try to reconnect with my family. It had been ten years since I'd lived anywhere near them and I guess I hoped that time and distance had worked some magic and we'd be one of those picture-book happy families."

He raised his dark brows. "Only if the book happened to be written by Edgar Allen Poe. Something along the lines of *The Fall of the House of Usher.*"

She smiled, but sadly. "I know that now. But earlier, coming back to Halford House seemed to be the ideal move, both personally and careerwise. Unfortunately, from the moment I arrived Dad was more distant than ever toward me. He actually seemed angry to have me around."

Garrett thought back to that first conversation he'd had with Art Halford. The man had seemed petrified of his daughter, so much so that he claimed he couldn't possibly tell her he'd sold the hotel. He'd even called her a jackal! But it had become obvious to Garrett that Shelby seemed more afraid of her father rather than vice versa.

Art's attitude struck Garrett as quite self-serving, an attempt by a bullying father to portray himself as victim. Whatever the truth, there was a serious perception and communication gap between father and daughter. There could be no doubt that Shelby had had a rough childhood, and her mother, detached and vague, couldn't have offered much support. Garrett's heart went out to her.

Shelby heaved a sigh. "When I first returned, I thought maybe I was overreacting, being too sensitive like I'd been as a child," she continued. "But it appears I was right about Dad being angry to have me back. He'd made plans to sell the place and when I showed up, I was nothing but an unwanted complication."

She sounded so dispirited, she looked so sad. She was hurting and Garrett hated it. He turned slightly, so he could gaze squarely into her hazel eyes. "Coming back to Halford House was an ideal move for you, personally and careerwise," he said firmly. "Because if you hadn't come, we never would have met. And I never would've had the chance to ask you to marry me. I'm asking you now, Shelby. I want you to marry me."

It took a moment for his bald statement to register, then she wasn't sure she'd heard him right. "It...almost sounded as if you were...proposing to me?" Her tone was as uncertain and incredulous as her expression. She waited expectantly for his joking reply, which was sure to follow her outrageous misinterpretation.

Instead, Garrett continued to gaze into her eyes, his own blue gaze somber and unwavering. "I am proposing to you, Shelby." There was no wisecrack, no droll smile. His voice was earnest and intense. "Marry me."

"That sounds more like an order than a proposal." Shelby tried to lighten the mood, to stall for time, while she gathered her shattered, scattered thoughts.

"Take it any way you want, but take it seriously, Shelby. Because I am very serious about marrying you. As soon as possible."

She abruptly stood, stumbling a little as she started to walk toward the water. "That's...that's very sweet of you, Garrett, but—"

"Sweet?" Garrett was on his feet beside her, catching her arm to halt her in her tracks. "I ask you to marry me and you say it's *sweet?"* His voice rose with indignation. "I thought I told you the last time you tried to label me as sweet, that I most definitely am not."

"It's not an insult, Garrett. Though you try to hide it and you vigorously deny it, you do have this caring, sweet streak in you that compels you to make grand gestures. A case in point—your purchase of the Blue Springs Resort so your little brother can be a golf pro there. And now you're offering to marry me because you feel sorry for me."

"I would never propose marriage to a woman because I felt sorry for her," growled Garrett. "I can list many reasons why I want to marry you but pity certainly wouldn't be included on the roster."

"What would be?" Her voice was not much more than a whisper. The moment she realized that he was serious about this marriage proposal, she also recognized how very much she'd wanted him to be. How much she wanted to marry him. The admission startled her, yet exhilarated her, too.

"We have a lot in common," Garrett began, taking her up on her request to list the reasons he might want to marry her. "The hotel business, for one. This past month we've both learned some things about the higher- and lower-price markets and we found that we share an interest in both. And we enjoy a lot of the same activities—movies, running, swimming, kite flying—"

"We've never flown kites together. That kite you bought last week never got off the ground," Shelby reminded him.

"Because the wind wasn't strong enough."

"Because it was cheap and poorly made, from one of those atrocious junk shops you love to patronize." She was grinning at him, her hazel eyes teasing. Her heart was pounding, her spirits beginning to soar. She was in love with him and he'd asked her to marry him! The crushing news of the sale of Halford House receded in the light of this incredible development.

"Okay, the kite was a dud, I concede the point. If I may continue . . ." He pulled her into his arms. "We're dynamite together in bed and what we have will keep getting better, Shelby. Out of bed, I enjoy your company immensely, even when we're fighting. In fact, I'd rather argue with you than make love with any other woman in the world."

He gazed down at her. "You're the only woman I've ever asked to marry me, Shelby. I'm tired of being single. This past month with you has made me realize how much I want to be married . . . to you, my baby. Say yes, Shelby. Say you'll marry me."

"Oh, Garrett!" It was a cry of joy tinged with just a touch of yearning. If only he'd added that he loved her to the list. If only he had opened with those three magic words, he wouldn't have had to make the list at all!

But his arms were around her, crushing her into him, his mouth was hot and urgent against her skin. He had asked her to marry him, he'd all but said that she was the only woman in the world for him. If that wasn't love...

Shelby lifted her head and smiled up at him, her eyes shining. "Yes, I'll marry you, Garrett." The expression on his face was all she needed to confirm the rightness of her decision. He might not have said the words, but Garrett McGrath loved her, she was sure of that.

It would be her pleasure to wring those three crucial, wonderful words out of him! And she would, too, however long it might take. Shelby was laughing when his lips came down hard on hers for a possessive, passionate kiss. She was certain that it wouldn't be very long at all.

At Garrett's insistence, the two of them left for Buffalo that evening. Shelby mildly protested the disorienting haste of their departure. She'd barely had time to announce the news of her engagement to her parents, and Laney was nowhere to be found. But Garrett was adamant about catching the evening flight out.

"It's time you met the family," he said firmly.

Shelby had known him long enough to recognize that his particular tone of voice when combined with the fierce glitter in his eyes and implacable set of his jaw, meant he would not be swayed from his decision. There was a time when she would have felt compelled to argue with him—it was not in her nature to allow anyone to feel omnipotent—but tonight she was feeling too mellow and too bemused to expend the energy.

She was engaged to be married! She replayed her parents' reactions in her mind as the plane landed in the rainy Buffalo night. Her mother—sweet and rather distracted as usual—had hugged her and warmly congratulated her on "finally finding a fine young man." Her father had first appeared incredulous, then laughed and slapped Garrett on the back.

"It's a done deal, then," Art Halford had said, and when Shelby questioned his rather enigmatic remark, her father had simply shrugged and wished Garrett good luck.

A limousine took them from the airport to the town house condominium that Garrett owned in one of the suburbs surrounding the city. Shelby was surprised by its unprepossessing size and decor. It did not look like the home of the president of a successful company. It did not seem like anybody's home at all. There were no personal touches or effects within; the place had the temporary, unlived-in atmosphere of a motel room.

Shelby told him so.

"I don't spend much time here," Garrett explained. "We'll buy our own place as soon as we're married. We can start talking to realtors and looking at houses tomorrow, if you want."

"I hadn't thought of buying a house," Shelby replied, wide-eyed. "I'm still getting used to being engaged."

"Well, you'd better get used to it fast because you aren't going to be engaged for long." Garrett swept her up into his arms and carried her up the narrow staircase to his bedroom. "I want to make you Mrs. Garrett McGrath as quickly as possible."

Ten

    ——

"Garrett's getting married?"

"A wedding! How exciting!"

"Now we know why you've been in Florida for so long, Garrett! Less to do with Family Fun than your own fun, hmm? That was a joke, big brother. Ha! Ha!"

"Uncle Garrett, can I be a flower girl in the wedding? I want to wear a rainbow dress and purple shoes."

Shelby looked from one McGrath to another as they, in turn, looked her over, directing their comments to Garrett. Shortly before noon, she and Garrett had arrived at the house where his mother and grandmother lived together with Devon, the twenty-six-year-old sister who was twice divorced, and Devon's two children, Pammy, six, and Petey, two.

Twice divorced. That came as a surprise to Shelby, who'd come to think that the McGrath clan personified family perfection as completely as they dominated the family motel business. Garrett hadn't mentioned that his younger sister had been divorced twice. Devon announced it herself upon her introduction to Shelby.

"On your last visits home, you never even mentioned that you were seeing anyone seriously, dear," Garrett's mother, Kate, chided him affectionately. She smiled warmly at Shelby. "I'm delighted to meet you, Shelby. I've been praying Garrett would find someone special to settle down with and I can tell just by looking at you, that you're the right girl for him."

"On the other hand, Mom also thought that Josh Alden was the right guy for me and look how that turned out," Devon interjected, grimacing. "We were married for less than a year and then he ran out on me while I was pregnant with Petey."

"Your mother is an optimist, Devon," countered Grandmother McGrath tartly. "She tends to see the best in people, even when it's not there."

"Can I be a flower girl, please, Uncle Garrett?" begged Pammy, hugging her uncle around the knees. "Please, please, please!"

"She wants to wear a beautiful long dress and toss flowers as she walks down the aisle," Kate McGrath said, smiling fondly at her granddaughter. "That's what a flower girl does, Pammy."

"No kidding." Pammy rolled her eyes.

"That child has a fresh mouth," old Grandmother McGrath muttered disapprovingly. "Reminds me of you as a child, Garrett. You were such a little smart aleck, I wanted to throttle you at times. You improved as you grew up, though," she conceded.

Shelby caught Garrett's eye and bit her lip to stifle a grin.

"Bet you can't wait to meet the rest of the clan," Garrett said dryly. "But it'll have to wait until tonight. Today, we're going to get the blood tests and apply for a marriage license. We can be married three days from now—on Saturday."

"Saturday?" Devon, Kate and Gran chorused together.

"*This* Saturday?" Shelby squeaked.

Garrett met her startled hazel eyes. "I told you we were getting married right away."

"We better go shopping for my flower-girl dress right now," Pammy advised.

"You can be a flower girl if you want, Pam, but this is going to be a very small, very simple wedding," Garrett decreed, his eyes still holding Shelby's.

"Oh, one of *those* weddings, where speed is of the essence," Devon drawled.

"The eight-pound preemie," recalled Gran. Her sharp blue eyes raked Shelby so thoroughly that she blushed. "Well, then, we have no time to lose. The sooner you two are married, the better."

"Garrett!" Shelby gritted through clenched teeth as he hustled her out of the family home. "I am *not* pregnant!"

He patted her arm. "I know, sweetie." He grinned rakishly at her. "But this time next month you will be."

Her eyes widened. They were sitting in Garrett's car, a blue-gray four door that was stylish and luxurious and a far cry from his tiny rental car. Suddenly she missed the cramped boxiness of that little car as much as she longed for their freewheeling days at Halford House.

But here in Buffalo, things were moving at an astonishingly rapid pace. "This is all happening too fast." Shelby spoke her thoughts aloud. "Garrett, I came to Buffalo with you to *meet* your family, not to marry in to it three days from now!"

"Why wait?" Garrett demanded. "I've never seen the point of a long engagement. You either want to get married or you don't. We both do, so we will. This Saturday."

Shelby's head was spinning. "Garrett, slow down. I wanted to enjoy our engagement and plan a wedding—not a huge one, but a nice one, a wedding to remember forever since I only intend to get married once. I thought we could have the reception at Halford House. I've dreamed of that since I was a little girl sneaking peeks at the wedding receptions in the ballroom. It will require some planning, but we don't have to own the place to..." She paused abruptly, to stare hard at him. "What's this about me getting pregnant within a month? We've never even discussed having children and suddenly you inform me that—"

"Don't you want kids?"

"I'm not the antimaternal career woman from hell that Laney has always painted me." Her face softened. "I'd love to have children. Two, maybe three." She smiled. "Definitely not nine."

"That's okay with me. Having nine kids is one McGrath legacy I don't care to repeat. In fact, none of us do."

"Thank heavens, we agree on something."

"We agree on a lot of things, Shelby. We've already listed why we're right for each other and how good we'll be together. Let's stop wasting time and get to it."

His refusal to even consider doing things another way annoyed her. And Shelby was not one to suffer her irritation in silence. "This is the way you run Family Fun Inns, isn't it? Once you've targeted an area, you blow aside all reasons to the contrary and just get to it. You're ensconced before the opposition knows what's hit them. The Blue Springs Resort and all those other places didn't stand a chance against you. Well, getting married and putting up a motel are two very different issues, Garrett, and I think you're confusing them."

"I am perfectly capable of separating business from my personal life, Shelby," Garrett said impatiently. "My corporate self is not my private self and I've never confused the two. As for the Blue Springs Resort, I'm sick of hearing about the place. It would suit me to never have it mentioned again."

"Well, that's unfortunate as well as impossible," Shelby retorted. "Since you own it, you're going to have to—"

Garrett took a deep breath. There were some facades that were no longer useful to maintain and this was definitely one. "I don't own the Blue Springs Resort, Shelby. I didn't buy it and I never said that I did," he said baldly.

She stared at him in confusion. "But Paul said... I thought...you certainly indicated that—"

"There have been some false assumptions about me buying the Blue Springs Resort, which I didn't bother to correct," Garrett interrupted, shrugging. "I was sure you'd jump all over them, Shelby. I'm surprised you haven't yet. Think about it. Why on earth would I buy the Blue Springs? Its niche was the high-end market and it has lost its value there. It's right next to a Family Fun Inn, in an increasingly touristy area that has cost the resort its exclusivity and its snob appeal. Even worse, the two properties would be competing against each other, which certainly wouldn't be profitable for us. I would never throw away the company's money—my family's money—on such a loser deal."

Shelby felt a chill run through her. He was smiling a shark's smile, his blue eyes held a predatory gleam. It flashed to mind that in all the time she'd spent with him, she had severely underestimated his strategic cunning and his manipulative skills. In the playful and sexy relationship that had developed between them these past weeks, she had considered herself his equal in every way. Sometimes she'd even felt she held the upper hand. After all, she was the one who had been born into a high-end hotel family and would inherit a famous exclusive resort. Garrett McGrath ran a thriving company, it was true, but it was at the low-end of the market and he'd built it from scratch, with no classy birthright to help him attain his position.

And achieving such success demanded qualities, strategies and tactics that someone born to the Halford House would not need to possess or even know about.

Suddenly she didn't feel quite so superior. Or even equal. It was as if she'd slipped down some metaphorical ladder and was hanging on by a shaky rung, while Garrett loomed far above her, poised to dislodge her completely. She shook her head, as if to dispel the image.

Garrett took her cold hand in his big warm one, lifting it to his lips and kissing her palm. "Forgive the lecture," he said, his gaze warm and affectionate. He displayed no signs of predatory sharkness now. "Sometimes I get carried away and think I'm giving a seminar in Business 204—Knowing

Your Market. I teach that as a night course once a year at the community college here," he added.

"I didn't know that," Shelby murmured. There was a lot she didn't know about him; she was just beginning to realize exactly how much.

"I donate my fee to the local children's hospital. I wanted to give something back to the community, you know? And I've been given plenty of opportunities to do so. Since Family Fun Inns has become so successful, the McGraths are sought after to serve on the boards of every charity and public service institution in the city."

Shelby pictured him sitting on various boards, a rich and powerful man directing funding and making important decisions, a major player with major clout in his hometown. It seemed so at odds with the man she'd come to know in Florida, the irreverent rogue in funny T-shirts who patronized junk shops and challenged her to raft races in the ocean and made wild sweet love to her for hours.

She tilted her head and gazed at him. He was wearing a Buffalo Bills jersey and jeans and he looked just like the Garrett McGrath she'd fallen in love with. She was being foolish, she admonished herself. She was just spooked by his unexpected rush for a wedding, a little unnerved at the prospect of meeting all those McGraths.

"What are you thinking?" Garrett demanded, pulling her close. He nibbled on her earlobe, his teeth worrying the small gold hoop earring.

"I guess I was thinking that I've underestimated you," she admitted. "I'm sorry."

"Don't be. I've been underestimated by others throughout my career," Garrett said cheerfully, completely without rancor. "I even encourage it. I've found that being underestimated is a priceless gift."

Shelby was shocked. "But I hate being underestimated! I've always considered it insulting."

"You have to make it work to your advantage." Garrett kissed her forehead, then set her away from him and started the car. "You've been rather insulated, honey. And if you want me to continue to shelter you, I'll be glad to do it. On the other hand, if you want me to teach you what I've learned in the trenches, I'll have fun doing so. Your choice."

"Here's my choice. I want to spend the day with you," she said softly. "I want you to show me around and for us to have fun together like we've been doing in Florida. And I don't want to talk about blood tests or licenses or weddings. Please, Garrett?" Shelby looked up at him, her hazel eyes pleading.

Garrett felt his heart lurch. It occurred to him that when she looked at him in that certain way and addressed him in that particular tone of voice, he would be unable to resist giving her whatever she wanted or doing whatever she wanted to do. It was a disconcerting thought. He had never been so captivated by a woman, so attuned to her wishes and needs. He'd always thought that having five sisters had immunized him against feminine wiles; whether charming or manipulative, he'd seen them practice firsthand and remembered what he had learned. Nothing had diverted Garrett McGrath from his chosen course of action until he'd met Shelby Halford.

He cleared his throat. "Have you ever been to Niagara Falls?"

Shelby shook her head and grinned at him. "Let's go."

There were myriad tourist excursions in Niagara Falls and Shelby and Garrett did them all, including the famous Maid of the Mist, a boat ride in the water near the thunderous cascade of the falls, the Cave of the Winds in which a wooden walkway led up and under the falls, and a heart-stopping ride in an aerial car high over the wild waters of the whirlpool. They stood on the rocks of Three Sisters Island near the swirling, dangerous rapids flowing directly over the falls. They ended their tour with a stop at the museum that preserved a meticulous record of all those rides over the falls, intentional or accidental, fatal or not.

"Disaster as entertainment. This reminds me a little of the hurricane museum in the Keys," Shelby said dryly. "Are you going to buy a T-shirt?"

"I have dozens from this area with every theme imaginable. But I'll be happy to buy one for you. You can wear it to dinner tonight. Mom invited the whole clan over for her specialty—takeout pizza from Luigi's. It's an Italian restaurant in the shopping plaza a few blocks from home."

"You're kidding, right?"

"About Mom's idea of a home-cooked meal? Nope. She's always hated to cook. Now she doesn't even pretend to try. But she loves getting the whole family together. Everybody will be there tonight except the three youngest. Aidan and Brendan are away at college and Caitlin is in veterinary school in Pennsylvania."

"So that leaves Glenn, Gracie, Fiona, Eilish and Devon." Shelby recited the names in one breath. "And you're each just two years apart," she added, awed by the length of the unbroken chain of siblings.

"Staircase kids, Gran called us. She also thought that Mom and Dad should have stopped with the first three G's. I remember her telling my father, 'You can't afford all these children.' But the folks went on to have the rest of the alphabet gang."

He swung the car off the main road into an open woodsy area. Shelby, turning her attention from their conversation to her surroundings, was surprised to find them heading through the open gates of a cemetery. She glanced questioningly at Garrett.

"I thought we'd pay a visit to those McGraths who won't ever be able to meet you," he said huskily.

He was bringing her to visit the grave of his father, Jack McGrath, Shelby realized. She was touched. She knew Garrett had adored his father, who had died far too young from complications of kidney disease. Garrett spoke often of his father, crediting him with having the idea of a motel chain that was visually fun and extra cheap, catering especially to families with children and not much money to spend for a vacation. Jack McGrath hadn't lived long enough to see his dream realized, the dream that had been achieved with astounding success by his eldest son and had benefitted the entire McGrath family.

Garrett parked the car and guided her among the headstones to the McGrath family plot, several feet away from a towering oak tree. "There's Grandfather McGrath—" he pointed to a headstone "—and my dad's older sister Mary, who never married, and here's my father, Jack McGrath."

Shelby gazed respectfully, noting the dates and the comforting biblical inscription. Her eyes flicked to the left of the headstone to a smaller one that had a baseball bat and glove carved into it along with the words Beloved Son. The name read Glenn McGrath and the dates of his birth and death were inscribed below it. A quick calculation revealed that he had been twelve years old when he'd died.

Shelby was stunned. Garrett had mentioned his sisters and brothers from time to time but he had never mentioned that one of them happened to be dead. She gaped at him, at a loss for words.

"I have trouble talking about it...his death. About him," Garrett said haltingly.

"Glenn," Shelby said his brother's name.

"Glenn," Garrett repeated thickly. "After all this time, it still gets to me. I guess that's why I rarely come here. I haven't been for years. Mom and Gran are here every Sunday without fail, though."

"Maybe coming here brings them some sort of comfort or peace," Shelby suggested quietly.

"I guess so. But it depresses the hell out of me. Still, I...I wanted you to see. To know."

Shelby put her arms around him and hugged him tight. "What happened to Glenn, Garrett?"

"He loved to play baseball." Garrett nodded toward the sad etchings on the tombstone. "He was good, too, a real competitor. From the time he was little, he could hit the ball farther and harder than kids who were a lot older than him." There was a note of brotherly pride in his voice. Shelby's eyes moistened.

"One night in July, a bunch of us neighborhood kids were playing ball in the street," Garrett continued. "Glenn ran after the ball, determined to get it so the hitter would be out. You can guess the rest. He ran right into the path of a car."

"Oh, Garrett," Shelby murmured sadly. "I'm so sorry."

Garrett nodded. "He was killed instantly. I saw the whole thing." He shook his head. "I can remember it as if it had happened yesterday. Glenn lying there, the driver, an older man, getting out of the car in hysterics. He hadn't been speeding but he didn't have a chance to stop. Glenn had just run into the street without looking."

"I can't imagine how horrible it must have been for you," Shelby whispered.

"Losing him was the worst thing that's ever happened to me. We were best friends, we shared so many interests. We were the two older brothers in a family with five younger sisters." He smiled slightly, reminiscing. "We used to tease the girls by barring them from our room. Mom had given birth to Brendan a month before Glenn was killed and we were so glad to have another brother. We told the girls we were finally starting to even the odds against us. Gracie was particularly incensed when Glenn and I would take the baby into our room, saying it was strictly for men only and girls were forbidden to enter. She would stand outside the door arguing how unfair it was and Glenn and I would crack up laughing."

"She took the bait every time, hmm? What a pair of older brothers you were."

"Yeah, we were a pair." He felt the old pang of loss but didn't allow it to linger for more than a few seconds. He'd learned long ago how to relegate the past, its sorrows and its joys, to a place in his mind that was accessed only when he chose and only for as long as he chose. He decreed that brief interlude to be over now. It was time to return to the present, a time he much preferred. He could influence and control the present.

Garrett's smile broadened, the stark sadness disappearing from his eyes. "I suppose it was inevitable that Grace would grow up to be a lawyer, dedicated to fighting sexist discrimination against women. She watches Family Fun Inns like a hawk, ready to nail us if we ever step out of line. So far we've met her standards, but other companies haven't and she zealously pursues them. Her husband Jeff is our general counsel and he believes the issue of sexual discrimination in the workplace has been exaggerated. Grace is always saying that he just doesn't get it. As you can imagine, the two of them have an interesting marriage."

"As interesting as living in a war zone," Shelby said dryly.

"Grace and Jeff fight like cats and dogs but they seem to thrive on it. They even had a baby last year. But don't worry, motherhood has not mellowed our Gracie's fervor for justice in the least."

"She sounds awfully formidable. Should I be scared to meet her?"

"Nah! Just complain about my T-shirt collection and she'll love you. Grace is always lecturing me on my tacky T-shirts. She thinks I should lounge around in designer polo shirts or crisp, preppy sport shirts. She actually bought me this awful plaid one once."

"She is courageous. Tell me about the others. I know their names but not much else about them."

They walked toward the car, their arms around each other. Shelby noticed that Garrett cast a brief glance over his shoulder at the McGrath headstones, then tightened his grip on her, determinedly hastening her to the car.

He filled her in on the others as they drove along the highway that had become congested with commuter traffic. "Fiona is very sweet, never raises her voice and never gets angry. She's an angel. Somewhat boring, but an angel. I think I already told you that she's married to Ray who designs and builds playgrounds and equipment. Their twins are Glenn and Sean. Which brings us to the letter E and my sister Eilish. Eilish is..." He paused, laughing. "How to describe Eilish? Well, her role model is Grace and they're a lot alike. Eilish is bright, fierce and dedicated to her work, which happens to be Family Fun Inns. All her drive and energy are devoted to the company. She wants to run it with me someday."

"Are you going to let her?" Shelby asked curiously. "Or are girls still barred from the room, according to your strictly-men-only policy."

"Ouch, I think." Garrett threw her a look. "You're going to hit it off with Eilish just fine."

"I've already met Devon and her kids," Shelby prompted.

"Ah, yes, Devon, the family underachiever. She used to ditch school regularly and hang around with an appalling group of losers. She married two of the biggest jerks I've ever met and I swear she did it because I warned her not to."

"And you were right about the jerks both times?" Shelby surmised.

"Naturally." Garrett sighed. "Devon loves her children, but she still has a lot of growing up to do. I've already told her that I'm picking out her next husband for her."

"Garrett McGrath, that's disgustingly paternalistic and patronizing! I bet your sister Grace read you the riot act when you handed down that edict."

"No, she didn't. She agreed with me. Devon drives Grace crazy—she calls her 'The Rebel Without a Clue.'"

"Poor Devon," Shelby murmured. "What about Caitlin and your two younger brothers?"

"Caitlin and Aidan are excellent students." The familiar note of familial pride was back in Garrett's voice. "She's studying to be a veterinarian and he's interested in becoming an environmental engineer. You already know that Brendan isn't much of a student but he sure can golf. The younger three still seem like kids to me," he added thoughtfully. "I don't know them as well as I'd like. I was out of the house and working during most of their growing-up years. I regret that."

He reached across the seat and took Shelby's hand. "It taught me a valuable lesson, though. I'm not going to work eighteen-hour days and be on the road four days a week while our own children are growing up. I don't want to miss those years with them. My dad was one of the best. He might not have made much money but he was always there for us.''

"I'm sure you'll be a good father, Garrett," Shelby said huskily.

"I also intend to be a good husband. And I'd like to get started right away.''

"I know. Like this Saturday." She was starting to get used to the idea, Shelby decided. Really, what was the point of a long engagement? She was certain that she wanted to marry Garrett. Especially after this afternoon. He'd shown her a side of him that she knew he had never revealed to anyone else. She felt both grateful and privileged and more in love with him than ever.

"Can we make the announcement to the family tonight at dinner?" Garrett pressed. "I can call in a favor or two and get that license so we can still be married on Saturday.''

"Could we compromise? We'll get married next week, in Florida. We can have a small informal reception at Halford House, with your whole family and mine there. I do want my parents and my sister to be at my wedding, Garrett, and I don't know if they can make it up here on such short notice.''

Garrett's mouth tightened. It was more than a compromise, it was a perfectly reasonable solution. From her point of view. But not from his. He was in full possession of all the facts; Shelby was not. She had finally been informed that he hadn't purchased the Blue Springs Resort, but she still didn't know who the buyer of Halford House was.

When she found out that it was him . . .

His breath hissed softly between his teeth. He'd broken some major rules by keeping her in the dark about the sale all these weeks and she was going to be furious when she learned the truth. And deservedly so, he admitted to himself.

But he intended to make sure he was married to her when she found out. As her husband, he would be in a better position to endure her wrath and weather the storm of her fury. Marriage conferred certain rights, both legal and emotional. Marriage provided ties that were necessary to sustain the bond between them during difficult times.

And telling Shelby that he'd bought Halford House and duped her into thinking otherwise, definitely qualified as a difficult time, Garrett thought grimly. He would need every right, tie and bond available to keep her with him, until she settled down and accepted the situation.

And she would accept it, he assured himself. Their marriage would thrive, despite this temporary problem. Why, they would probably even have a good laugh about the whole thing someday.

Garrett refused to let himself consider any other outcome.

"I don't want to wait until next week," he said, his voice low and urgent. "I'll arrange for Laney and your parents to fly up for the wedding. I promise you that they'll be here. If you want to honeymoon at Halford House, that's fine with me, but I want the wedding here. On Saturday."

Her old self would've immediately taken umbrage and fought tooth and nail for her case, Shelby thought. There was a part of her that still wanted to, an almost reflexive urge to go down fighting for her cause. She suspected that Garrett was much the same way—perhaps even more so because he was long used to calling all the shots while she only aspired to it.

But she was a woman in love whose lover was desperately eager to marry her. How angry could one really be in those circumstances? And though he had yet to say he loved her, Garrett's impassioned rush to the altar proved beyond a doubt how very much that he did.

A glow spread through her, warming her with joy. Garrett couldn't wait to make her his wife and he wanted to do it in the city that he considered his home. His business was here, his family was here, the two of them would be living and raising their children here.

Why shouldn't they be married here?

And if Saturday was a bit sooner than she might have chosen, well... Marriage did call for compromise, didn't it?

"Saturday," she repeated.

Adrenaline pulsed through him, as if he'd just emerged victorious from a round of intricate, uncertain and highly volatile negotiations. He supposed he had, in a way. "Saturday can't come soon enough for me, sweetheart," he said with heartfelt sincerity.

Shelby was touched. He really did love her, she was certain of that. "I love you, Garrett." She snuggled as close to him as the car's deep bucket seat and shoulder strap would allow.

She hoped he would take her cue and respond with his own pledge of love. But she wasn't too upset when he didn't. She was a firm believer in the old actions-speak-louder-than-words school of thought, and Garrett's actions—his intense determined courtship of her during the past weeks at Halford House, his urgency to marry her, and especially the way he'd shared his most poignant, personal memories with her during this afternoon's impromptu trip to the cemetery—were all the actions of a man deeply in love.

Eleven

Shelby decided that meeting the McGrath clan en masse was not unlike booking a convention into a hotel and then juggling the demands of the multitudinous delegates during their stay. She was grateful for the stamina her hotel training and experience had provided in dealing with large, raucous groups. She'd handled trial lawyers' conventions and state political party caucuses at the Casa del Marina so she felt equipped to keep up with the outspoken, opinionated McGraths.

Certainly every McGrath, including the two brothers-in-law, seemed to have an opinion on everything, which they expressed spiritedly, interrupting and correcting and arguing with each other as they wolfed down slice after slice of Luigi's deep-dish pizza. Empty pizza boxes and bottles of soda piled up in the kitchen as the youngest and smallest McGraths ran around underfoot, as animated and noisy as the adults.

Shelby observed the McGrath family dynamics with fascinated interest. Garrett was clearly in command; even old

Grandmother McGrath deferred to him, if not somewhat grudgingly. After everybody had their say on the matter at hand, Garrett issued the final word, and though there might be further arguments, all seemed to concede that his word was law.

"After all, Garrett's always right," Devon relayed to Shelby while a debate raged on about whether or not to re-think the current restriction on stocking free shampoo in Family Fun Inns. Garrett had already vetoed the idea. "I'm the only one who's ever actually defied him and I did it *twice*. And both times my marriages blew up in my face, just like Garrett said they would. Don't think that lesson was lost on the rest of the family! Then, of course, he's never made a wrong move in the business, so that's heightened his aura of infallibility. Around here, whatever Garrett says goes."

Whatever Garrett says goes. The words resounded in Shelby's head. It called to mind the way he'd set their wedding date. It had been business as usual for him; he'd is-sued his decree and probably wasn't surprised in the least that she had capitulated. He hadn't expected any other out-come.

But if Garrett McGrath thought he was always going to have the final say in his marriage, he was in for a big sur-prise. Shelby's resolve was mixed with amusement, and she smiled contemplatively. She would enjoy teaching him that compromise was a game for two players.

"You look like the cat who just figured out how to un-latch the bird cage," Garrett murmured into her ear. He had crossed the room to stand beside her, and he draped a pos-sessive arm around her waist. "I've been watching you," he said. "And I'd offer you a penny for your thoughts but I think you'd raise the bid to a dollar."

"You'd be right." Shelby leaned her head against his shoulder and savored the hard, warm strength of his near-ness.

"You're exhausted," Garrett said solicitously. "And no wonder. I dragged you all over Niagara Falls today and then threw you into the middle of a McGrath family—"

"Gathering," Shelby finished for him.

"Very diplomatic of you, honey. I was going to say fracas."

"Not to worry, Garrett. Today didn't require half the endurance of a dark and stormy night at the Seagull Motel."

They smiled, sharing the memory.

Garrett kneaded her waist with his fingers, discreetly, yet sensuously. "If we were to spend the night there again, we'd pass the time a lot differently," he promised.

"What? No candy slam dunks and songfests? Whatever would we do for fun?"

"As if you didn't know." His blue eyes were burning into hers. He wanted to be alone with her. He'd spent the evening watching her move easily among his family. That she could hold her own with them he'd never doubted, and he had enjoyed seeing her prove him right. Not even Gran's sometimes curmudgeonly remarks threw her. Growing up with Arthur Halford's alternating disinterest or wrath, coupled with her experience at placating cranky hotel guests, was good preparation for anything a McGrath might dish out.

His body tightened with the desire she always roused in him, and always would. It had been hours since he'd held her and kissed her the way he wanted to, hours since they'd lain in bed, so passionately and intimately joined.

He leaned down and lightly kissed her lips. "Let's go home," he said softly.

Shelby's body tingled as her blood simmered with anticipation.

"Aha! You two are planning to sneak out!" Eilish exclaimed gleefully, almost pouncing on Shelby and Garrett as they edged their way toward the door. "Well, you can't leave just yet, Garrett. I want to discuss my proposal to install swimming pools in all the Florida Family Fun Inns. People expect pools when they vacation in Florida. It's hot and the kids want to swim and—"

"We've considered putting in pools from the inception and decided against it every time. So one more time—no pools, Eilish," Garrett said with a finality Shelby knew well. She suspected all the McGraths did, too, but Eilish wasn't about to concede defeat.

"But, Garrett, look, I've got it right here." Eilish waved a folder that she desperately tried to shove into Garrett's hands. He deftly avoided taking it.

"I've worked up a—" Eilish tried again, only to be firmly cut off by her older brother.

"With pools come liability insurance rates that sky-rocket annually," Garrett said with a weary patience. "There are pool maintenance costs and lifeguards to be hired, not to mention the initial construction costs, all of which will drive up the prices of our rooms, thereby defeating the very purpose of our existence."

"But, Garrett, don't say no until you've seen how affordable my proposal—"

"No, Eilish." Garrett sounded bored.

"Garrett, at least listen to her," Grace spoke up, her McGrath blue eyes flashing. "Give her a chance to—"

"Hmm, which part of no are you two having trouble understanding?" Garrett asked dryly.

Shelby observed the exchange, picturing a much younger Garrett and his brother Glenn chortling in their room as their enraged sisters demanded admittance and were told no. Things hadn't changed much, it seemed. The girls were still being told no, and it struck Shelby as patently unfair. Eilish was both Garrett's sister and his employee. Setting aside the family relationship, it didn't hurt to at least listen to underlings before telling them no. She'd learned that old chestnut in an entry-level course in hotel management.

It suddenly seemed important that she take a stand to prove her own independence, to both herself and Garrett. He was such a strong man, it would be easy for a woman to get into the habit of deferring to him. Until it no longer occurred to her to think for herself at all.

"We'll take your proposal and look it over tonight," Shelby said firmly, taking the folder from a visibly stunned Eilish. "Won't we, Garrett?"

"No, we won't," Garrett replied pleasantly.

"Oh, yes, we will." Shelby nodded her head. *She* was not one of his kid sisters pounding on that locked door.

The McGrath sisters exchanged glances, then broke into laughter. "Aren't you afraid that Garrett is going to grind you into dust for daring to defy him?" Devon asked with relish.

"He just might, you know," Grace warned, her tone wryly acerbic. "And then vacuum you up with merely a shrug."

"They're only teasing, Shelby. Garrett would never do such a thing," Fiona put in loyally. "He's the most wonderful brother in the world."

They left with Eilish's folder clutched firmly in Shelby's hand. "I hope you don't mind that I insisted we take this with us," she said tentatively, her hazel eyes wary. She didn't want to argue with him, but...

"Mind? I thought it was a move worthy of the most savvy public relations agent!" Garrett enthused. "You managed to win my sisters' respect, admiration and loyalty with one small gesture. Family Fun Inns could use a PR person with your skills."

"I didn't do it to ingratiate myself with your sisters," Shelby protested. "We really are going to look over this proposal tonight. I happen to agree with Eilish—your motels in Florida ought to have swimming pools."

"Sure, we'll look at it, baby." Garrett's eyes swept over her in an unmistakably suggestive and thorough once-over. He grinned rakishly. "We'll look at it in bed, after we're too worn-out to do anything else."

"I don't think you're taking this matter with the seriousness it deserves, Garrett McGrath," Shelby said primly. She affected an expression of disapproval worthy of Miss York herself. But when Garrett made a decidedly lewd but hilarious proposition, she couldn't keep from laughing, totally eradicating her Miss York guise.

* * *

The moment they entered Garrett's condo, he picked Shelby up and headed toward the small staircase. The folder fluttered to the ground as she linked her arms around his neck. Shelby didn't worry about it. They could look at it later. Meanwhile, she was aching for Garrett's touch.

"Remember the first time I carried you?" Garrett said, his lips curving into a teasing, reminiscent smile. "You gave me a lecture designed to daunt a less persistent lover."

"But you weren't daunted," Shelby reminded him, clinging closer. "You were a very persistent lover."

"I always intend to be." He lowered his lips to hers. Shelby let out a tiny, blissful sigh and melted against him.

And then the doorbell rang. Twice, three times. "Ignore it," muttered Garrett. But when it continued to sound, and the ringing was followed by a heavy pounding, he sighed and reluctantly set Shelby on her feet.

"I guess I'd better at least see who's there," he said. "That doesn't mean I'll open the door."

But when the ringing and the pounding was accompanied by a loud, "Shelby, Shelby, open up. It's Paul. I know you're in there. I've been waiting, watching for you to come back. I have something very important to tell you."

"Paul?" Shelby was bewildered. "What on earth is Paul Whitley doing here?"

Garrett strode ahead of her and opened the door a crack. "This is a bad time, Whitley," he said, his voice cold and hard. "Call my secretary in the morning and set up a meeting with me tomorrow."

"I didn't come here to see you, I came to see Shelby and I'm going to see her now," Paul argued, shoving against the door. He was no match for Garrett's strength. If Shelby hadn't been there to intercede, Garrett would have successfully closed the door, shutting Paul Whitley out.

"Garrett, you have to let him in," she exclaimed, tugging at Garrett's arm, trying to pry loose his grip on the door. "Paul, what are you doing here? How did you find us?" Her heart contracted. Perhaps he had been sent to find them. "Is there something wrong at Halford House? My parents, Laney, are they—?"

"I had no trouble finding you," Whitley snapped. "It was certainly no secret that you'd gone to Buffalo with McGrath and when I got here, I looked up his address in the phone book."

Garrett grimaced. "Remind me to have myself unlisted in the future."

"Paul, please tell me what's going on," Shelby cried. "Do you have bad news about my family?"

"I suppose that depends on whose point of view and what's considered bad news," Paul said sardonically. "Your parents are fine and your sister is fine. Oh, Laney is particularly fine. I realize now that she's one of those women who will *always* come out ahead, no matter what happens to everybody else around them."

"What are you talking about, Paul? Garrett, please, move aside and let him in! If you don't, I'll go outside to talk to him."

At that threat, Garrett reluctantly allowed Paul to enter. His usually impeccable clothes were rumpled, the smooth bland features of his face twisted with emotion. And Shelby perceived that emotion to be primarily fury. "Paul, what's wrong?" Long experience with men in similar straits led her to bluntly add, "Did Laney break up with you?"

"Break up with me? Hah!" Paul's face contorted with rage. "That's a tactful way of putting it. Far more tactful than simply saying that she dumped me cold for Oliver Tate!"

"Oliver Tate?" Shelby echoed, truly shocked. "But he's years older than Laney—*decades* older! Why, he's old enough to be her father!"

"And much, much richer than her father," growled Paul. "She told me last night that she was flying out to Idaho with Tate. They flew out first class, the two of them *and* her dogs! He'd given her this mega-size emerald friendship ring. Some friendship! When I think of her with him, I . . . I—"

"It does kind of make you sick," Shelby agreed sympathetically. "But I think we can both guess why she did it, Paul. Oliver Tate bought Halford House and Laney has always considered it home. She obviously thinks that—"

"Laney knows damn well that Tate did not buy Halford House," Paul interrupted harshly. "We found out the day you left to come here who the *real* buyer is." He looked accusingly at Garrett.

Garrett held his stare but said nothing.

"It's not Oliver Tate?" Shelby repeated, confused. "Then who?"

"You still haven't told her?" Whitley glowered at Garrett. "When did you plan to break the news, McGrath? After you told her you *hadn't* bought the Blue Springs Resort?"

"Shelby knows I didn't buy the Blue Springs," Garrett said coolly.

Shelby looked from one man to the other, a sickening dread causing a knot to swell in her chest, growing bigger and bigger until she could hardly breathe. There was only one conclusion she could draw from all of this. "You're the buyer," she gasped, staring at Garrett as if she'd never seen him before. "*You* bought Halford House!"

Of course! It was so obvious! Even as she comprehended the news, Shelby scorned herself for not realizing it sooner. Of course, Garrett McGrath had bought Halford House. She should have known from the ingratiating way her father had been toadying to Garrett that something unusual was in the works. And when she thought of the way Garrett had moved into cottage 101, while being allowed access to every department and all information pertaining to the resort, pieces of a puzzle she'd hardly bothered to ponder fell into illuminating place.

As if Arthur Halford would grant anyone the "privileges" he'd allegedly granted Garrett McGrath. Letting him hang around to learn, up close and personally, the high-end of the hotel/resort market! She couldn't believe her own naiveté in swallowing such a whopper of a lie. Garrett had been there because he was the owner of the place. It was his right to have his questions answered upon his command, to go wherever he pleased within the grounds, to do whatever he chose with the property. He could paint all the doors alternating colors of the crayon box if that's what he wanted. Halford House belonged to Family Fun Inns!

An intense fury, stronger and fiercer than anything she had ever known, began to uncoil within her. *Garrett had bought Halford House!* She'd been living in a stupid dreamworld for the past weeks, and the stunning force of reality was as painful and dizzying as an unexpected punch in the stomach.

Garrett watched the range of emotions play across her face, from incredulity to shock to burning rage. He knew her so well that he could identify each one, almost following her thought patterns as she worked everything out.

"Shelby," he began, then paused, realizing that he had no idea what to say next. He'd envisioned breaking the news to her slowly, gently and subtly, on their honeymoon. In his imaginary scenario, she accepted the truth because she was his wife, so madly and passionately in love with him that nothing else really mattered.

But one look at the hurt and horrified expression on her face told him that he'd been living in a fantasy world. Married or not, Shelby was not going to take this matter lightly.

"Why?" Her voice was a hoarse rasp. "Why did you do it, Garrett?"

"Why did I buy Halford House?" Garrett stalled for time. He knew the answer to that particular question very well. He'd outlined the reasons to his staff within the company and discussed his plan with friends in the industry. He'd even presented his reasons to Art Halford, who found him credible—and rich—enough to sell him Halford House. "There were several reasons, all of which—"

"Don't you dare try to sidetrack me with your corporate prevarications!" Shelby cut in wildly. "I want the truth, although I realize that might be difficult for a lying weasel like you!"

Her heart was pounding, her head was pounding, too. A violent sense of betrayal welled up within her, rocking her as intensely as her rage and the awful sense of her own sheer stupidity. The combination was deadly. For a moment or two she felt almost nauseated from the powerful force of her emotions. That would be all she'd need, she thought grimly. To faint or throw up, right in front of Garrett McGrath and Paul Whitley.

She hated both of them, Shelby decided, her temper reaching flash point. She hated Garrett for his dishonesty and deceit, and Paul for, well, for being here and telling her of Garrett's dishonesty and deceit. For the first time ever, she truly understood the old custom of killing the messenger of bad news. If she were of a homicidal bent—and at this moment, she was somewhat sorry that she wasn't—she would have slaughtered Paul right along with Garrett.

"Why didn't you tell me that you'd bought Halford House?" she raged at Garrett.

How could I have been so incredibly blind? she asked herself at the same time. Her own answer appalled her. She'd been blind because she'd wanted to be. She was living, breathing proof that the stupid old cliché "love is blind" wasn't so stupid or out-of-date, after all.

"Damn, I should have figured it out," she said fiercely, talking to herself instead of the two men who were watching her. Paul was visibly wary and nervous; Garrett's expression was totally unreadable. His mouth was firm and straight, his blue eyes hooded, giving nothing away. His very inscrutability further infuriated Shelby. At least Paul was afraid of her!

She began to pace the floor, too wired to stay still. "After all, your presence at Halford House was *another* false assumption that you didn't bother to correct—and that I didn't pick up on. Like your buying the Blue Springs Resort."

Another sharper stab of pain reflected in her hazel eyes. He'd had a perfect opportunity to tell the whole truth when he'd told her the partial truth about the Blue Springs. Instead he'd chosen to continue his deception, his lie by omission. "But my stupidity is my own fault, isn't it? I should have jumped all over the illogical reasons that—"

"I deliberately misled you, Shelby," Garrett cut in quietly. "I had no intention of letting you find out the truth until I was ready to let you know."

His bald admission scalded her. "You're a manipulating, lying snake!" A manipulating, lying snake whom she'd fallen deeply in love with—and had even agreed to marry this Saturday! "And I'm the most gullible fool in the universe."

Depression rolled over her in a crashing wave, supplanting the wild, primitive high that had been energizing her. Hot tears filled her eyes. "I'm getting out of here," she announced, breaking into a run. She would rather be thrown over Niagara Falls in a cardboard box than cry in front of Garrett McGrath!

"Shelby, wait!"

Garrett came after her. She knew he would. Whatever game he was playing did not include her walking out on him. She was halfway down the front walk when he caught her arm, spinning her around and halting her in her tracks. "Look, I know what I did was wrong," he said, and there wasn't a trace of either flippancy or executive command in his voice. Garrett McGrath sounding contrite, she scorned. Now that was a first!

"But if you'll give me a chance to explain, I can clear up this misunderstanding and—"

That was when she drew back her hand and slapped him full across the cheek. "This was no misunderstanding, you . . . you arrogant creep! You intentionally duped me!"

Garrett gingerly rubbed his cheek. Her slap packed a real wallop. He supposed he deserved it. Gran and his sisters would certainly say so, with the possible exception of Fiona, who might cut him some slack. Garrett sighed. He deserved no slack. "Yes, I did," he admitted. "And I'm sorry."

"How far did you intend to carry your little charade? And why the insistence on a wedding?" Her voice trembled and she despised herself for it. "I can understand you getting a sadistic kick at playing me for a fool these past weeks, but there was certainly no reason to ask me to marry you—"

"There was a very good reason." Paul Whitley had joined them. His mouth was twisted in a smile of bitter triumph. "You haven't heard the entire story yet, Shelby. You see, your father refused to sell him Halford House unless he married you. The whole deal is contingent on it."

Twelve

Shelby gaped at him, too shocked, too wounded to utter a sound. But her mind was racing, flashing back to certain scenes that she now reassessed with stunning clarity.

She remembered the time her father had sent her to Garrett's cottage with the folder containing the irrelevent brochures, disguised as important business. She'd been touched at his matchmaking attempts, but Art Halford hadn't been matchmaking at all—he'd been trying to make a sale! And she had literally fallen into Garrett's arms that day, had fallen in love with him.

"You don't know what you're talking about, Whitley." Garrett's voice rose with anger and indignation.

He was angry and indignant because he'd been found out, Shelby concluded, feeling sicker by the minute. He was undoubtedly seething with frustration because he had been so close to successfully pulling things off. Oh, it all made sense to her now. Garrett's insistence on a speedy wedding, his determination to rush her to the altar. She'd believed that he was in a hurry to make her his wife because he loved her. In truth, he was eager to secure his rights to Halford House, and that couldn't happen until he put a wedding ring on her finger.

It's a done deal! Her father's response to the news of her quickie engagement to Garrett echoed in her ears. She had thought it a bit odd, but then, nobody knew better than she that her father was not a sentimentalist. A done deal, indeed! That's exactly what it was, or would have been, come Saturday.

"I know very well what I'm talking about, McGrath! I know the full story!" Paul Whitley's sharp retort cut across her bleak reverie. "Laney told me everything, right after she announced that she was leaving with Oliver Tate." He turned to Shelby, his expression petulant. "Laney said your father figured you would drive away every eligible man on your own and so he arranged to land a rich husband for you while building a retirement nest egg for himself."

Shelby thought she would die from the pain that was resounding through her. And then, mercifully, she went numb. "I see," she said flatly. "Well, that explains it all, then."

"It explains nothing because it is nothing but a barefaced lie," Garrett said, his voice as hard as his blue eyes. "Think it through, Shelby. You know me well enough to know that—"

"No, Garrett," she said distantly. She was suddenly, wonderfully cool and remote, untouchable by everything around her. "I really don't know you at all." Squaring her shoulders, she continued down the walk, her head held high.

"I rented a car, Shelby," Paul said helpfully, falling into step beside her. "I'll drive you where you want to go."

Shelby fought the temptation to brush him aside like a bothersome gnat. But she had to forgo the pleasure, since she could use his assistance. "All right, Paul. You can drive me to the airport. But first, I'd like you to go inside Garrett's lair and get my purse and my suitcase. Would you do that for me? I would appreciate it so much." To her own ears, she sounded as fake and phony as Laney weaseling some poor chump. And to her utter amazement, Paul nodded his consent.

But he didn't have to do it. He'd started for the door as Shelby sat stiffly in the front seat, staring out the windshield at the flickering streetlight when the back door of the car was opened. Shelby jumped, startled. Garrett placed her suitcase and her purse in the back seat.

"This isn't over, Shelby," Garrett said in calm, measured tones. "Not by a long shot."

She wanted to scream some scathing retort, but pride called for her to keep her dignity intact. It was the only thing she had left, she reminded herself, her heart and her pride having been decimated by Garrett McGrath, hotelier-fiend. "Give it up, Garrett," she said with a world-weary sigh. "I'm not going to marry you, so you won't get Halford House."

"If you want to break into the high-end of the market, go buy the Blue Springs, McGrath," Paul jeered, sliding behind the wheel.

They drove away into the night. Garrett, standing on the sidewalk with his hands thrust into the pockets of his jeans, watched until the car was long out of sight.

There wasn't a direct flight to Miami that night, so Shelby and Paul took a series of available flights south, first to Pittsburgh, then to Charlotte, and finally into Miami, arriving in the early hours of the morning, a few hours before dawn streaked the sky.

Paul made a few stabs at conversation during the long, disjointed trip. "I'm really sorry all this happened, Shelby," he said with credible sincerity. "I'm sorry about everything. When we left California for Florida, I thought our friendship might develop into something deeper." His voice and his expression turned bitter. "It might have if it hadn't been for Laney. I was transfixed by her. But I blame her, not myself. What man could resist a beautiful woman like Laney?"

If he expected a reply from Shelby, none was forthcoming. She knew of one man who'd easily resisted Laney. Garrett McGrath. And then she remembered why he'd been so immune to her sister—because Laney hadn't been offered as part of the hotel package that she, Shelby, had been included in.

Shelby steadfastly refused to acknowledge the spasm of pain ripping through her. She couldn't deal with this now, she told herself sternly. She wouldn't.

They rented another car and drove to Port Key and Halford House. Shelby tiptoed into her room, taking care not to wake her parents. She was relieved that she hadn't called to tell them about the Saturday wedding; at least she wouldn't have to explain the abrupt cancellation. And then she remembered that the sale of Halford House was contingent on her marriage and that her parents—or certainly her father—probably knew all about Garrett's wedding plans.

All the agony of betrayal, of falling in love only to learn that the man she loved didn't love her at all—that he'd been using her to gain a hotel for his burgeoning empire!—burst out of the shackles she'd temporarily put on it. She no longer had the balm of anger or numbness to keep the terrible hurt at bay.

Lying alone in the twin bed in the dark privacy of her girlhood room, Shelby began to cry.

"What are you doing back?" Arthur Halford greeted Shelby the next morning in the kitchen as he and his wife sat down to breakfast. "Where's Garrett?"

Shelby shrugged and managed a brittle smile. "In Buffalo, I guess. I came back last night with Paul." She was dressed in gray shorts and a gray T-shirt for her morning run on the beach. The color suited her dreary spirits.

"I didn't hear you come in. Did you sleep well, dear?" her mother asked.

"Yes, Mom," Shelby said, lying outright. Anyone looking at her could tell she'd had a terrible night, but then, who in the Halford family had ever really looked at Shelby? She hadn't slept at all last night and it showed. There were dark circles under her eyes and her face was pale and drawn. She'd cried for hours, until her throat ached and her eyes burned from the stinging salt of her tears. Her eyes were red and swollen, her nose puffy and her voice hoarse from her sore throat, all evidence of her prolonged crying bout.

Her parents made no comment about her appearance, but her father was quick to demand, "When is Garrett coming back?"

Shelby poured herself a cup of black coffee, inhaling the bracing aroma and taking a bolstering gulp before replying, "I hope he never comes back, Dad. I found out about the plot to sell Halford House, so the game is over."

"What game?" her mother asked blankly.

At least Mom wasn't in on the plot; Shelby was grateful for that. "Oh, Dad and Garrett had some deal where if Garrett married me, he could buy Halford House," Shelby said with feigned nonchalance.

"Garrett told you *that?*" Arthur Halford demanded incredulously. He was gaping at her, appalled.

"Relax, Dad, Garrett didn't let the cat out of the bag. It was Paul. Laney told him the entire plot."

Mrs. Halford looked upset. "I suppose Paul also told you about Laney and Oliver Tate. Your father and I are stunned! But we knew she was serious about him when she insisted on taking her dogs with her. We have no idea when she'll be home."

"Who can blame Tate for being enchanted with Laney?" Art snapped. "He'll do the right thing by her, I'm sure. Meanwhile, what's this nonsense that Whitley has been spreading?"

"Laney fed Paul some tale about the sale of Halford House being contingent on my marriage to Shelby." Garrett himself walked into the kitchen, still wearing the same jeans and shirt he'd had on last night. He looked tired and haggard, his usually alert blue eyes were bleary from lack of sleep.

FAMILY FEUD
181

Without waiting for an invitation, he sat down at the table, reached for a mug, and poured himself a cup of coffee.
Shelby stared at him, feeling too exhausted and too weak to
react to him at all.

"Why would Whitley say that? Why would Laney?" Art
demanded. "It's not true."

"And Laney, that angelic little Girl Scout always tells the
truth, doesn't she?" Garrett said, his tone cool with sarcasm. "She would never make up some devious lie to explain away a man's preference for her sister over her. And
Whitley was willing to believe what Laney said. He'd been
dumped and his ego was bruised—he was probably glad to
find a fellow reject in Shelby. He couldn't wait to come
running and spread the misery." His eyes met Shelby's.
"Does any of this sound plausible to you?"

"It sounds plausible to me," Arthur Halford said. "Except the part about Laney being devious. She has a very
playful sense of humor, you see. She was probably just
joking with Whitley and that idiot took her seriously."

"Well, so did I." Shelby stood. "I guess that makes me
an idiot, too."

"Yeah, it does." Garrett stood, also. "Glad to hear you
admit it. Come on, let's get out of here. We have a lot to talk
about." He reached for her hand.

Shelby backed away. "I have nothing to say to you."

"Because you think I have to marry you to get Halford
House?" Garrett growled. "I already own the place. I
bought it weeks ago. The bill of sale was signed the day I
arrived in Florida. The date is on the title of ownership, if
you want written proof."

"That is absolutely true," Art affirmed, nodding. "But
I asked him for a little time to, um, break the news to you.
After he saw you for the first time, when you came into my
office that day, Garrett asked me to let him break the news
to you himself. He wanted to pick the time and place."

"And when was that going to be?" Shelby asked crossly.
She was immediately annoyed with herself for speaking to
him. After telling him she had nothing to say to him, she

had intended to keep it that way. So much for her vow of silence.

"It was going to be after we were married. Probably on our honeymoon," Garrett said bluntly. "I knew you'd take it badly so I hoped to...to..." He paused, frowning, and glanced at her parents. "Can we continue this discussion privately?"

"You can't throw my parents out of their own kitchen!" stormed Shelby. "Or is this your way of throwing your weight around as official owner of Halford House? You want to make sure everybody knows that you own everything on the grounds and that your sacred word is law?"

"No one is throwing us out, dear. We were on our way to your father's office, anyway." June Halford tucked her arm in her husband's, and headed out the kitchen door. Art was visibly eager to go.

Alone, Garrett and Shelby faced each other. "They're gone now, so go ahead and say it," Shelby continued furiously. "You wanted to wait until our honeymoon because you thought I'd be so besotted by your overwhelming sexual technique that I wouldn't care that you'd lied and—"

"You already were overwhelmed by my sexual technique, remember? If that was my plan, I'd have told you everything the first time I took you to bed. Or any time thereafter. But I wanted to be married to you when you heard about the sale, Shelby. I wanted you to know that Halford House was yours because you were married to the new owner."

She stared at him, somewhat nonplussed. "You're going to have some smart, smooth answer to whatever I say, aren't you?" She scowled. "You are a slick one."

"While I know you don't mean that as a compliment, it's a helluva lot better than a lying, manipulative snake and an arrogant creep. I sense my stock is rising."

"Don't you dare." Tears filled her eyes, even as her lips were quivering into a wholly reluctant smile. "Don't you dare try to make me laugh."

"I want to make you laugh." He walked around the table to stand before her. "I want to make you happy, Shelby. What I never want to do again, is to make you cry." He traced the dark shadows under her eyes with his thumbs, noting her reddened, swollen eyes with remorse. "I love you, Shelby."

"I thought you did," she whispered achingly. "But when Paul..." Her voice broke off as she stifled a sob.

"Whitley!" Garrett said with contempt. "He blew any chance he might've had to ever work for me." His blue eyes narrowed to angry slits as he thought of the trouble and misery Whitley's spiteful trip had caused. "Forget Whitley, I already have." Not that he would ever forgive the other man's interference. It was not the McGrath way.

He reached for Shelby, pulling her into his arms. She went stiffly, but did not fight him. Her body, though physically exhausted, had taken over for her mind. And she craved his nearness, the warm strength of him that she feared she would never experience again.

He held her pressed tightly against him, lightly stroking her hair. "You feel so good in my arms," he murmured huskily. "We only spent one night apart but I missed you so much it felt like a part of me was missing." The feel of her firm, rounded breasts crushed against him stirred his body into hard, urgent arousal. "I have the key to cottage 101. Come with me, sweetheart."

"Just like that?" Shelby's voice was still raspy. She felt what was happening to his body and it evoked a piercing, sensual response deep within her own. But the lingering pain of last night's misery had not yet been dispelled. "You want me to go to bed with you and forget all about what's happened?"

Garrett sighed. "Who said anything about going to bed? I asked you to come to the cottage with me. We can talk privately there. You'll agree that we do have a lot to talk about?"

She drew back a little and the glance she gave him was almost admiring. "You really are slick, McGrath."

"Thank you, I think." He took her hand and led her out of the house, down the path to cottage 101. "But it's not a good thing to be too, uh, slick. I need a woman around who won't let me get away with it all the time."

"You have your grandmother and at least four of your sisters to do that."

"Yeah, but ultimately, they end up kowtowing to me. They've fallen victim to my infallibility myth. There are times when I believe it, too, and that's not good. I need a woman around to remind me that I can be wrong at times. And when I'm wrong, I'm wrong in a big way."

She gazed up at him as they walked hand in hand. Despite what had gone on between them last night, at this moment all she could feel was an overpowering sense of rightness at being with him. She loved him, it was that simple. Whatever arguments or obstacles arose between them was secondary to that powerful, elemental fact. And Garrett loved her. He was trying so hard to be penitent. Suddenly she was both touched and amused by his attempts to humble himself for her.

"For example, the way I handled this Halford House mess was inexcusable," he continued glumly.

A sudden smile broke over her face, lighting her weary hazel eyes. "I assume you're talking about the *misunderstanding?*"

Garrett stopped in his tracks and stared down at her. He instantly comprehended her understanding, her forgiveness.

"Shelby!" He breathed her name adoringly. In a spontaneous burst of relief and joy, he picked her up and swung her around once, twice, three times, before setting her back on the ground. "I love you so much," he groaned, holding her tight.

Shelby closed her eyes and hugged him back. "I know. I love you, too, Garrett."

"And you'll marry me?" he pressed urgently. "As soon as possible?"

She nodded. "Although now that the big secret is out, we don't have to follow your desperate timetable. We can have the wedding and reception here at Halford House a few weeks from now. Your whole family can fly in and stay here. They really ought to inspect the newest McGrath holding, don't you agree?"

"I most definitely agree, my darling," Garrett said, scooping her up into his arms.

"And I think we need some time alone, just the two of us, before adding a little McGrath to our family," Shelby continued. Why stop now? She was on a roll here.

"Agreed." He kissed her, sealing the bargain, then proceeded to carry her all the way to cottage 101.

*   *   *   *   *

JINGLE BELLS, WEDDING BELLS:
Silhouette's Christmas Collection for 1994

Christmas Wish List

*To beat the crowds at the malls and get the perfect present for *everyone,* even that snoopy Mrs. Smith next door!

*To get through the holiday parties without running my panty hose.

*To bake cookies, decorate the house and serve the perfect Christmas dinner—just like the women in all those magazines.

*To sit down, curl up and read my Silhouette Christmas stories!

Join *New York Times* bestselling author Nora Roberts, along with popular writers Barbara Boswell, Myrna Temte and Elizabeth August, as we celebrate the joys of Christmas—and the magic of marriage—with

JINGLE BELLS, WEDDING BELLS

Silhouette's Christmas Collection for 1994.

JBWB

MILLION DOLLAR SWEEPSTAKES (III)

No purchase necessary. To enter, follow the directions published. Method of entry may vary. For eligibility, entries must be received no later than March 31, 1996. No liability is assumed for printing errors, lost, late or misdirected entries. Odds of winning are determined by the number of eligible entries distributed and received. Prizewinners will be determined no later than June 30, 1996.

Sweepstakes open to residents of the U.S. (except Puerto Rico), Canada, Europe and Taiwan who are 18 years of age or older. All applicable laws and regulations apply. Sweepstakes offer void wherever prohibited by law. Values of all prizes are in U.S. currency. This sweepstakes is presented by Torstar Corp., its subsidiaries and affiliates, in conjunction with book, merchandise and/or product offerings. For a copy of the Official Rules send a self-addressed, stamped envelope (WA residents need not affix return postage) to: MILLION DOLLAR SWEEPSTAKES (III) Rules, P.O. Box 4573, Blair, NE 68009, USA.

EXTRA BONUS PRIZE DRAWING

No purchase necessary. The Extra Bonus Prize will be awarded in a random drawing to be conducted no later than 5/30/96 from among all entries received. To qualify, entries must be received by 3/31/96 and comply with published directions. Drawing open to residents of the U.S. (except Puerto Rico), Canada, Europe and Taiwan who are 18 years of age or older. All applicable laws and regulations apply; offer void wherever prohibited by law. Odds of winning are dependent upon number of eligibile entries received. Prize is valued in U.S. currency. The offer is presented by Torstar Corp., its subsidiaries and affiliates in conjunction with book, merchandise and/or product offering. For a copy of the Official Rules governing this sweepstakes, send a self-addressed, stamped envelope (WA residents need not affix return postage) to: Extra Bonus Prize Drawing Rules, P.O. Box 4590, Blair, NE 68009, USA.

SWP-S994

Dark secrets, dangerous desire...

Lovers DARK AND DANGEROUS

Three spine-tingling tales from the dark side of love.

This October, enter the world of shadowy romance as Silhouette presents the third in their annual tradition of thrilling love stories and chilling story lines. Written by three of Silhouette's top names:

LINDSAY McKENNA
LEE KARR
RACHEL LEE

Haunting a store near you this October.

Only from

Coming in September from Joan Johnston

CHILDREN OF

Remember the Whitelaws of Texas from Joan Johnston's bestselling series *Hawk's Way?* Well, they settled down to have three sweet and innocent little kids. Now those little Whitelaws are all grown up—and not so innocent! And Silhouette Desire has captured their stories in a very sexy miniseries—*Children of Hawk's Way*.

Why is gorgeous rancher Falcon Whitelaw marrying a widowed mother who'd rather sleep with a rattlesnake than him?

Find out in Book One, *The Unforgiving Bride* (SD #878), coming your way this September...only from

If you are looking for more titles by

BARBARA BOSWELL

Don't miss this chance to order additional stories by
one of Silhouette's most distinguished authors:

Silhouette Desire®

#05651	THE BABY TRACK	$2.75	☐
#05685	LICENSE TO LOVE	$2.79	☐
#05787	TRIPLE TREAT	$2.99	☐
#05821	THE BEST REVENGE	$2.99	☐

(limited quantities available on certain titles)

TOTAL AMOUNT	$	
POSTAGE & HANDLING	$	
($1.00 for one book, 50¢ for each additional)		
APPLICABLE TAXES*	$ _____	
TOTAL PAYABLE	$ _____	
(check or money order—please do not send cash)		

To order, complete this form and send it, along with a check or money order
for the total above, payable to Silhouette Books, to: In the U.S.: 3010 Walden
Avenue, P.O. Box 9077, Buffalo, NY 14269-9077; In Canada: P.O. Box 636,
Fort Erie, Ontario, L2A 5X3.

Name: _____

Address: _____City: _____

State/Prov.: _____Zip/Postal Code: _____

*New York residents remit applicable sales taxes.
Canadian residents remit applicable GST and provincial taxes.

SBBBACK2

Silhouette®